Mr. Suicide

Praise for Nicole Cushing's *Mr. Suicide*

"...a work of brutal and extreme horror... disturbingly graphic content..."

—*Publishers Weekly*

"This tale of a damaged and murderous child is the most original horror novel I've read in years. Cushing's prose is rapid-fire, grisly, and passionate."

—Poppy Z. Brite, author of *Exquisite Corpse* and *Lost Souls*

"Novels don't come much more transgressive than this one, folks. Got a taboo? Watch Nicole Cushing grin while she dances all over it. In other hands that might be reason enough for the witty *Mr. Suicide* to exist. But this is more and better than that—a truly nightmare world, richly imagined, told to us in a canny, subversive second-person voice that makes you, the reader, the hero of this tale, like it or not. That it also manages to be ultimately life-affirming is yet another wonder."

—Jack Ketchum, award-winning author of *Off Season* and *The Girl Next Door*

"Nicole Cushing uses her sharp and confident prose like a surgical instrument to dissect both her characters and our emotions. *Mr. Suicide* is horrifying and harrowing, but just as much for the emotional devastation it causes in the reader as for the violence and depravity—as well as the twisted humor—it portrays. This is horror fiction that leaves marks."

—Ray Garton, author of *Live Girls* and *Sex and Violence in Hollywood*

Mr. Suicide

A Novel of the Great Dark Mouth

Nicole Cushing

WORD HORDE
PETALUMA, CA

First Edition

ISBN 978-1-939905-11-6

A Word Horde Book

To the memory of Alfred Schnittke (1934-1998)

I

Like everyone else in the world, you've wanted to do things people say you shouldn't do.

How many times in your life have you wanted to slap someone? Really, literally strike them? You can't even begin to count the times. Hundreds. Thousands. You're not exaggerating. You're not engaging in… whatchamacallit? Hyperbole? You're not engaging in hyperbole.

Maybe the impulse flashed through your brain for only a moment, like lightning, when someone tried to skip ahead of you in line at the cafeteria. Then it was gone and replaced by the civilized thought: *You can't do that. Not out in public.*

But you've had the thought.

It's not just you, either. On TV, you hear about people in New York shoving each other out of the way for cabs. On TV, you see news stories about people stampeding over each other to get a much-prized, heavily-discounted Christmas gift. You imagine their teeth gritted in primal struggle as they compete for temporary control over things. Everyone wants to be top dog.

Yes, you've wanted to slap the shit out of people. You've wanted to punch people, too.

Hell, at more than one point in your life you've wanted to

kill someone; *really, literally* kill someone. That's not just an expression. Not hyperbole.

No reason for shame. Everyone at least considers murder, at some point (though few would readily admit it). There's a reason it's illegal. Why would there be a universal prohibition against it, if there wasn't a universal yearning that had to be reined in?

To be more specific: the urge has arisen three times, so far, in your eighteen years.

The first person you wanted to kill was your mother. You were ten at the time. She'd assigned you the chore of cleaning the bathtub. You looked at the cylinder-shaped box of Ajax, and noticed it said to call Poison Control if you ingested it. That's when you realized you had a weapon. Actually, the first thought you had was to use it against yourself. (Yes, you contemplated suicide at age ten—you were precocious). But then you realized you needn't off yourself, especially given that your mother was the one who deserved death.

Why had you wanted to kill her?

She was obnoxious. Yeah, sure, that's not sufficient reason to kill someone, but it's easier to explain it all if you start there. When you enrolled in elementary school and, naturally, made friends, she yammered on and on about how sternly she disapproved of them. You were her precious little boy, and she wanted you all to herself.

She was cruel. Okay, this is a bit closer to a justification. When you were in middle school and taking sex ed, she told you that you'd never grow into much of a man, because your father sure wasn't one. She'd told you that your father couldn't please her in bed, and so you'd never be able to please a woman, either. She'd said, "Those sorts of things run in families."

When she'd said "things", she'd gestured toward your crotch.

She was vile, that way. Offensive. Filthy-minded. And yet, by some bizarre twist, conservative Christian dogma managed to coexist with all the vulgarity in her head. She prevented you from going to the movies, saying they were a bad influence. She censored your reading material, weeding out anything she deemed too close to "demonic". *The Lord of the Rings* was "demonic". Zombie books were "demonic". She went over your room with a fine-toothed comb for contraband. If she found what she was looking for, she confronted you about it. She screamed. She slapped.

She never drank a drop of alcohol or, to your knowledge, indulged in drugs. No one in your family did such things, to your knowledge.

But she was insane. Aggressively insane. She was drunk on rage, and when the bender could no longer sustain itself, she crashed and awoke the next morning with a hangover of depression. She bitched about her dissatisfaction with her lot in life (you, your father, and your brother were trotted out as prosecution exhibits A, B, and C). She never shut up. You were her youngest child, and as you went into the latter years of high school, she seemed to grow ever more morose and overprotective. Tried to keep you to herself. She frowned on you leaving the house for any reason not connected to school work. By then, your social skills were so rusty that, most of the time, you complied without argument.

These are only a few of her crimes. What you've detailed so far is not frivolous, but even more will be revealed. After the totality of her transgressions are presented in detail, all will agree you were justified in wanting her dead. Hell, if the Pope had been aware of all her crimes, even he would've nodded his little beanied head with slow, grave resignation and declared: "Yes, that bitch has to die."

And yet, you decided to spare her.

You wanted her dead, but didn't want to get caught. Besides, there were other ways to be rid of her. Maybe, you told yourself, you could leave the day you turned eighteen. On April 22, 2015, you'd move as far away as you could. You counted down the years until adulthood, the way a prisoner counts down years on a sentence.

Looking back, you're not certain you made the right decision. Had you killed her when you were ten (and gotten away with it; done it in such a way that everyone thought it was an accident or sudden illness), then everyone would have been free.

Your father would have spent the requisite year or two mourning, then started openly dating the co-worker you're pretty sure he'd had an affair with. You have three older siblings—a brother ten years older than you, a sister thirteen years older than you, and a brother fifteen years older than you. The brother ten years older than you never married, but your other siblings did. Had you slain your mother when you were ten, you would have saved them from the embarrassing scenes she made a few years later, at their weddings. And if your mother hadn't been around to make embarrassing scenes at their weddings, they wouldn't have stopped visiting. They would have called. They wouldn't have seen you as nothing more than an appendage of her. They would've answered your emails, because they wouldn't have thought their responses would be forwarded on to her. They wouldn't have cut off all ties with you.

The brother who's ten years older than you (the one who didn't marry) devolved to a state of idiocy. Your mother berated him until she broke him, and he was reduced from a man to a shard of one. He commuted to college, so he wouldn't disappoint your mother by moving out. When college was done, he commuted to graduate school. Then after graduate school, he broke down.

He graduated at the very worst point of the recession. He'd chosen an impractical master's degree. He could find no work within easy driving distance. One day, he began sobbing and hid under his bed. You were there, looking into his room from the hallway. Through the open door. You tried talking to him, but he wouldn't answer. So what could you do, except watch the whole thing with fascination? It *is* a fascinating thing, to be there the exact moment a mind crosses the threshold from precarious stability to full-blown madness. You imagine it's like watching a butterfly emerge from a cocoon. The old, gray protective wrapping falls away to reveal the creature's true, colorful nature.

Or maybe it's more like watching a woman give birth (you wouldn't know, for sure, you've never seen a woman give birth; the closest thing you've watched were birth scenes on TV or films, but it seems like an apt metaphor). He was sweating and bawling and writhing under the bed. "Puuuuush," you wanted to say. "Pushhhhh and *let the madness out*. Let it out, and then let's you and me do what we should have done a long, long time ago. Let's go mad, together. Let's commit the act of madness that would have stopped you from going mad. Let's pussssh a steak knife into dear ol' Mom's throat!"

But you didn't say that. You didn't say anything, for a long, long time. The scene took your breath away. It was a good five or ten minutes before you could tear your eyeballs away from it, before you could decide what to do.

Even though your parents could plainly hear the crying and thrashing under the bed, you had to draw their attention to it. ("Look at the mad butterfly coming out of his cocoon," you could have said. But you didn't. You weren't that poetic, in the moment. You said something along the lines of, "Hey, don't you hear that?")

Your mother sat on the sofa in the living room and pretended that it wasn't happening. Your father waddled over to the scene, fidgeted, and scratched his head. "He's kind of a weird kid," he said, "ain't he?"

Dad was overwhelmed by it all. He'd spent too many years under your mother's thumb. He wasn't sure how to proceed without her permission. She'd decided to ignore the scene, and to do otherwise would contradict her. He didn't have the balls to contradict her. He was a softie.

You wouldn't think he'd be that way, given his background. Blue-collar hick, all the way. Worked on the assembly line at the Ford plant. But he was a blue-collar hick who happened to find his mother dead of a heart attack when he was thirteen. He'd told you about it once—how she was all blue and shit when he found her. You think that probably made him the way he is—all sensitive, when it comes to women. Kind of a door-mat. Probably traumatized by the whole thing. Scared that if he ever had cross words with a woman, she'd keel over on him.

So he became a wimp. When he was in his early twenties, in the army, his buddies used to call him "Ajax" because your mother had gotten so pissed at him that she'd flung an Ajax container at him and nailed him in the forehead. That cut made a scar. But he never left her.

He wasn't much of a role model for you, now, was he? When he wasn't busy being a doormat, he was busy packing on the pounds with ice cream and candy. Or living vicariously through the younger, more athletic men playing baseball on TV.

Your brothers would have been better off if you'd killed your mother. Your sister would have been better off if you'd killed your mother. Your father would have been better off if you'd killed your mother.

And yet, you failed to follow through with the murder. Which makes it all the more funny, when you think about how things sorted themselves out.

But more about that later. You've gotten a little ahead of yourself. Jumped from one year to another, to suggest the general *flavor* of your troubles. People have always said you're jittery, and you think they say that because you try to tell them everything in one frantic breath. Better to slow down, if you can. Take things step by step.

II

Of course, you didn't earn good grades in high school. Ten-year-olds who plot homicide and contemplate suicide rarely grow into teens who make the Honor Roll.

Of course, you had no friends in high school. Those friends you'd acquired almost effortlessly in first grade became acquaintances you only spent time around sporadically in fifth grade. Those acquaintances became virtual strangers by high school. Oh, on the first day of high school they said hello to you when you said hello to them. But after the first week, they stopped saying hello to you when you said hello to them. They only nodded politely. By December of ninth grade, you'd say hello to them and they wouldn't even acknowledge your presence.

It ached when that happened. It really did. Your efforts to connect with them *invariably* led to aching.

So you stopped trying to connect with them.

So you became something… other. Something… different. Alone and apart, a creature whose mind had gone places his peers' minds couldn't even imagine. Didn't you, in a way, stop being a child when you began to plot homicide and contemplate suicide? The most intense moments of your life, up to that point—those moments when you'd engaged in such plotting and contemplation—defined you, changed you, burned whatever bridges existed between you and others your own age. Yes, everybody considers murder, even if just in a fleeting thought. But few do so, in any serious way, before puberty! (And as for suicide—most people serve at least two decades of their incarceration in flesh before they consider the option of shuffling off their mortal coil).

So, at ten, the most interesting conversations you had were internal ones; those conversations between you and your suicidal thoughts. You had so many of these conversations, it was like suicide was a *person*. ("Why not today?" Mr. Suicide asked you. "It's summer, and there's no school and you're stuck at home with your bitchy mother and a carton of Ajax.")

***

It would be that way for the next several years. It's hard to explain, but you weren't sure if Mr. Suicide was just in your head, or if you'd actually *heard* him. You only know that he hung around you. Frequently.

When you were eleven, Mr. Suicide asked you: "Why not today? Everyone made fun of you when you were chewing on a pen so nervously that ink gushed out and stained your mouth. This is surely the sort of fuck up from which there is no recovering. Do the honorable thing and let's put an end to your life now. Fall on your sword. People will respect you for admitting you are without value. Well, maybe they won't respect *you*. I guess what I mean is they'll respect *the honesty*, you know? Why not now? Why not now?"

Because I'd get it wrong, you thought. *With my luck, I'd just hurt myself real bad, instead of killing myself. I might put myself into a coma instead of dying.*

"You say that like it's a bad thing!" Mr. Suicide said. "Comas have a bad reputation, but I bet you'd dig it. You'd exist, but you wouldn't exist. If you went into a coma, you wouldn't *know* you were in a coma. It would be pretty much like death, I think, except you'd still be breathing. Consider the advantages: *you'd* get to stop thinking and feeling. *Your parents* would get to avoid all the hysterics of a funeral. It's a win-win!"

You asked Mr. Suicide where he got his information. *I wouldn't be* aware *I was in a coma, huh? Do you know that for sure, or is this more of a* guess *on your part?*

He had nothing to say in response to *that*. Dead silence. You had a hunch that meant Mr. Suicide was making the whole thing up. So you didn't kill yourself. Because, what if this was a prank Mr. Suicide was playing on you? (Lots of people pulled pranks on you. Just the week before this conversation, Terry Whitlock—one of your old friends from elementary school—swore up and down that Tracy Rosenswie had a crush on you and wanted you to hold her hand. When you tried, she hit you in the stomach.)

***

When you were twelve, Mr. Suicide asked: "Why not today? You got a hard-on in class and some of the popular kids saw it and laughed. They kept asking if you were queer for the history teacher—old, yellow-toothed, stoop-backed Mr. Winnick. Why not now? Why not now?"

Because, you thought, *the school just held an assembly about suicide. The people talked about how it hurt those left behind. They brought in the family of that twelve-year-old in Paducah who did it two years ago.*

"That?" Mr. Suicide said. "Puh-lease. You're telling me *that* little propaganda show has convinced you to slug through the misery?"

You felt embarrassed when he called you out that way. He made it seem like you were just another slack-jawed yokel conned by a slick sales pitch. *You're outnumbered. You're the only voice telling me to do it. There are lots of voices saying not to. One by one, the family members came up and told everyone not to do it. The father started things off. He offered no reasons why we shouldn't do it. His entire talk was just two dozen repetitions of lines like "Don't do it," "It's a very bad idea," "It's a stupid idea," and so on. I'll admit, that part wasn't very convincing.*

Then the mother started to give her talk about the reasons suicide was a bad idea. By that point, the assembly was getting restless. The novelty of all this suicide shit was fading. The other kids slumped on the bleachers. Some of the biggest dickheads whispered dirty jokes or made farting sounds. They made it a little hard to focus and this was the only time during the school day when focusing seemed important. About three minutes into her talk, the mother disclosed what she saw and heard when she went into her "little boy's" room.

"I'll never forget how d-dark his hands were and how pale the rest of—" She could go no further before succumbing to a wave of hard sobs. The kind that shake shoulders. "I'm sorry, boys and girls," she said, "I thought I could do this but I, I can't." When she began to hyperventilate, the father had to go up and retrieve her.

Next came the brother—athletic-looking and wearing Marine Corps dress blues. He pounded his fists on the podium and said that if anyone in that gymnasium even thought about it, they "damned well better tell the guidance counselor".

"Did you?"

Did I what?

"Tell the guidance counselor."

No, because I'm not going to kill myself, no matter how much you try to convince me to.

"Hard head. Okay, tell me more about this assembly."

There was a collective gasp in the gym when the curse word echoed off the walls. It was the only time in school when anyone was allowed to say "damned" from the podium. (The brother was a hero of Afghanistan who had been given a medal for fighting for our freedom. He was home on leave. No one—not even the principal—was going to stop him from cussing. He could have said "fuck" and "cocksucker" and still been allowed to keep talking).

It made for good theater: the cussing was probably the part that saved the assembly from descending into chaos. It made the student body pay attention. No more fart sounds. No more whispered jokes. It gave the anti-suicide message a certain flair. It made it cool.

He said life was too precious and sacred to toss away like that. He went on to say that suicide (which he, and all the rest of his family, pronounced "sue-sad") was a permanent solution to a temporary problem.

"He was a big, fat liar, then," Mr. Suicide said. "We've been goin' through this since you were ten. How fucking *temporary* does that sound."

Things might get better when I move out of the house.

"More like *if* you move out. Look at that brother of yours. The one who went nuts."

But my oldest brother and my sister both made it out. It's not impossible.

"You moron. You really don't get it, do you? They made it out *because they're the oldest.* Your mother let them go because she had two younger ones still left to cling to. She managed to hold on to your older brother, and you can be sure she isn't going to let you go without a fight, either."

Maybe, but if it's a fight she wants, I'll be up for it.

Mr. Suicide sighed. "I'll still be hanging around you, then, too. I'll be hanging around and telling you: 'I told you so.'"

***

When you were thirteen, Mr. Suicide asked: "Why not now? Have you looked at yourself in the mirror lately? Greasy hair. Thick glasses. Pimples. Dude… pimples. You've got so many it looks like you came down with measles."

That would be a dumb reason to kill myself, you thought. *Everyone gets pimples. Even football players. No. Big. Deal.*

"But then again, kiddo, your face is a bit more blemished than theirs. And even the most pimply of football players can still get laid, you know. As for you… well… my guess is that even in your dreams, girls turn you down. You don't even get wet *dreams*, do you? You get blue ball dreams, instead."

You really know how to be charming, don't you?

"I know how to cut through bullshit, and that's just what I'm going to do. I'm not going to mince words: you're one fucking ugly looking nerd of a kid. C'mon, I'm not telling you anything the kids at school haven't already told you a billion times. What names do they call you?"

It's none of your business.

"What names do they call you?"

Shut up.

"What *names* do they call you?"

I'm not giving you the answer.

"Why… because it hurts too much to even say? Are they *that* bad?"

They call me Trash Ass. It's not even all that bad of a name. It's just stupid.

"And why do they call you that?"

It doesn't make any difference, does it?

"Why do they—"

Get out of my head!

"Only after you tell me. Not before."

Leave. Leave now!

"You don't have the power to expel me, flesh-thing, so I think I'm staying put right here in your brain for awhile. I want to hear you tell the story of how you got the name Trash Ass. Maybe it's not the name itself that bugs you, but rather how that name *came about*, eh? I have a hunch that there's something in the story of *how the name came about* that you need to face. I want to hear you tell the story, and *then* explain to me why you keep refusing me."

I'll tell it, but then you have to go.

"Sure, if you'll tell it, I'll eventually go. If you don't tell it, I'll keep tormenting you and I won't eventually go. I'll keep tormenting you until you kill yourself because that will be the only way to be rid of me."

You relented. It seemed like the lesser of two evils.

Okay, okay… There was one week in lunch when the teachers punished some kids who had started a food fight by giving everyone assigned seats. It was awful. They had us all sitting at tables according to alphabetic order, which meant there was one of the worst jocks close by. His dad was the gym teacher, so he pretty much got away with whatever he wanted to do. He was pissed at having to sit next to me. Pissed, I suppose, at having to suffer any inconvenience for his actions. He was so unused to being called on his behavior. (In fact, he was one of the main players in the food fight).

On Monday and Tuesday he hit me in the shoulder a few times when the teachers weren't looking. Then, after punching me, he pretended *to punch me* dozens *of times. If I flinched, he'd laugh and then hit me twice—harder than he ever had before. He would say: "That's two for flinching, faggot." Then he'd laugh some more.*

There were two other popular kids at the table who laughed with him, and a couple of unpopular girls there who looked like they just wanted the whole thing to be over. One of them was this disabled girl who went around school in heavy crutches. She put her head on the table throughout the entire ordeal.

By Wednesday, the punching game must have gotten old for the jock and his friends. So when I showed up in my assigned seat, I felt something soft and mushy collapse under my butt. It smelled like sour milk and rotting meat. I looked down and saw white liquid had stained my crotch.

"Oh my God," the jock wailed. "He's a homo. He just sat down next to me and came in his pants! I don't want to sit next to no homo. Nuh-uh!"

There was a brown paper lunch bag on the seat. It was old and it was smelly and it contained a half-full container of sour milk and a bologna sandwich that must've been in the trash for a week. I knew the jock didn't crawl into the dumpster himself to get it. He must've had accomplices who did the dirty work.

Mr. Suicide took on a know-it-all tone. Half-lecturing, half-ridiculing you. "They *always do* have accomplices to carry out the dirty work, kiddo. And it doesn't change when you get older. The jock will one day be behind a desk at the Pentagon or at an oil company or at a health insurance conglomerate, and he'll make some self-serving decision and force underlings to carry it out with dirty work. That's the nature of the world. The people who are at the top of the ladder in high school are usually the ones who stay at the top of the ladder throughout life. The ones, like you, who are at the bottom of the ladder in

high school usually stay at the bottom of the ladder throughout life. Hey now, speaking of ladders, wouldn't this be a good
night for a hanging?"

I'm not at the bottom of the ladder. I'm smarter than all of them,
and they know it. I just happen to live in Louisville, Kentucky,
and so I just happen to be surrounded by the sorts of kids socialized
in such a shit pit. When I graduate, I'll go to Chicago or New York
or L.A. I'll surround myself with other smart people, with people
who like books. It'll get better.

"It doesn't get better. It stays the same—or, hell, gets worse.
Life is like a movie that starts out shitty. Humanity is like an
audience in the theater, sitting there telling themselves that it's
gonna get better. Hoping against hope. And when it *doesn't* get
better, you folks can't admit to yourselves that you've wasted
your time sitting through crap. So you lie to yourselves and
cling to some small supporting performance or unique camera
angle that you can use as proof that you *weren't* wasting time.
That's what humanity's like: always trying to convince itself that
breathing isn't a waste of time." Mr. Suicide took on a mocking
falsetto: "'It'll get better!… It'll get better!' Ha! Repeat after me:
It doesn't get better. It doesn't get any fucking better."

I'm not ready to say that yet.

"Sheesh, kiddo. This is almost enough to convince me that
I'll *never* sway you my way. Let me try to extend my theater
metaphor a little, to improve your understanding. Have you
ever noticed how, in the theater, you'll laugh at unfunny jokes
just because everyone else is laughing? That's an example of
what I like to call consensus reality. Everyone has agreed that,
for that moment, the unfunny joke deserves a laugh. Laughter, in a crowd, is a reflexive social instinct. Tell the same joke
to yourself, at home, and you probably won't laugh. You may
even groan at how lame it is.

"Life's the same way. When you're in the midst of a crowded city, you have all kinds of people telling you—either in their words or their actions—that there are some very important, very meaningful things going on with their lives. And so it becomes contagious. Society forces you to absorb—almost by osmosis—the idea that life has meaning. The hierarchical nature of your species makes you try to prove that your life is *even more meaningful* than that of your fellows. Self-deception is programmed into your species. The advocates of hope believe it to be a feature. I believe it to be a bug.

"What do you get out of lying to yourself? Hmm, kiddo? You're a smart person, explain it to me."

I'm not *lying to myself. You're the liar. You make it sound like everything's going to stay the same. Any moron can tell that's not the case. When I graduate, I won't have assigned fucking seating in a cafeteria. I won't be forced to be in the same room as jocks. I think you're forgetting that I have a second older brother, besides the one who lives at home. He went on to become a lawyer. He'll never have to take lip from another jock, ever again. That's the privilege of being smart. He's going to be the boss of the jocks, not the other way around. Now leave. Go away. I have work to do. I have a shit pit to escape.*

***

When you were fourteen, Mr. Suicide asked you: "Why not now? There's an algebra test today. You haven't studied for it and when you flunk, your mother's gonna go bananas. You could write a note and make it look like an equation for her to solve. You could write: '14X = suicide. Solve for X, bitch. Solve for fucking X'! On the back of the note, you could write the correct answer: 'X = one year of living with a psychobitch mother!'"

That would be overly dramatic, you replied. *If I do it, I don't want to be dramatic. I don't want to leave a note. Notes are for girls and faggots. If I do it, I'll do it in such a way that there won't be any mistaking the fact that it was a suicide. I would hang my-self—that's plenty unambiguous. The proverbial picture worth a thousand words. That picture, alone, would say to whoever found me: "Look. I didn't want to be here."*

"Good thinkin'," Mr. Suicide said. "There's some rope in the garage. The little machine that controls the door opener is mounted to the ceiling. You could probably get a ladder and hang yourself from that."

If I do it, I'm not going to do it over a fucking algebra exam. In fact, Mr. Suicide, if you think I'd do it over a fucking algebra exam, then you don't know me very well at all. If I killed myself over the test, then that would imply that I gave a fuck. And the whole point is: I don't.

"You'll care when your mom finds out."

No, you insisted, *I won't. It's only one class. Besides, I still have an A in Mr. Chin's class.*

"You like Mr. Chin, don't you? He's different from all the other teachers, isn't he?"

Of course he is. He's another reason I keep on going. I think I'd actually miss his class, if I was dead.

"English, pffff! What good is that going to do you out in the cruel, hard world, eh? You going to impress people in job interviews by reciting 'To be or not to be'?"

Maybe. Maybe I could be a teacher, like Mr. Chin.

"Is he your role model, kiddo?"

It sounds stupid when you say it that way.

"Is he?"

Why does it matter? What business is it of yours?

"Answer the question!"

Okay… jeez… Yes! All right? Yes, I guess you could say that I want to be like him. He's smarter than my mom and dad. He knows about stuff they don't.

"Of *that*, I have no doubt."

He isn't all uptight like all the other teachers. He's not like a teacher at all. He's more like my friend.

"Do tell… "

He tells me about cool stuff. Stuff Mom and Dad have no interest in.

"Stuff like sex?"

No, you moron!

"Sorry, kiddo. 'Stuff' is awfully ambiguous. Can you be a little more precise? Just what does your teacher-friend tell you? When does he take time away from his busy instructional schedule to shoot the shit with you?"

My English class is kind of weird. We have the first half of the class, then lunch, then the second half of the class. Instead of eating lunch down in the cafeteria, with all the other kids, I eat up there with him.

"I see. Sort of a class-tucked-away-*inside*-the-class, you might say. Are you the only kid up there?"

No, but I'm probably the only kid who has *to be up there.*

"Care to explain?"

Now you're playing games.

"Beg your pardon?"

You know *why I* have *to be up there. It's part of the reason why you sought me out in the first place. Eating lunch down in the cafeteria makes me miserable. I see the tables where all my old friends sit. They have lots of new friends, now (people more popular than I am). I feel, in some ways, like I'm already dead. So I have to be there. Now, Andrea Matthews and Rachel Copeland are there, too. They're popular kids. They don't* have to *eat their lunch up there. They eat up in the room with Mr. Chin because they like talking to him, too.*

We talk about books and movies and stuff. Not the kind of things everyone knows about, but these odd ones. Once, he showed us all a documentary about this place called Jonestown, where everyone drank poison Kool Aid, on purpose, because the guy in charge told them to. That was pretty funny, because I was drinking Kool Aid out of a thermos when we were watching it. Funny, but also kind of badass. Then he told us about this one really, really old movie. It wasn't even shot in color—it was black and white. It was called Freaks. *That was pretty intense, for an old movie. Just like with the Jonestown documentary, we watched it together on his laptop over two or three days during lunch. It wasn't as cheesy as I'd expected it to be. Then he introduced me to* another *black and white one.* The Seventh Seal. *He lent me a copy and let me watch it on my laptop at home. He said he thought I was ready for it. He said that, after the Jonestown movie and* Freaks, *I should be ready for just about anything.*

"I bet your mother would have blown a gasket if she'd known you were watching that! It's not exactly good Christian family entertainment!"

I kept the volume down on my laptop and brought it back in to him the next day. I wouldn't dare keep it for longer than overnight. She's good at snooping.

"Was it worth the risk of bringing it into the house?"

I liked it. You were in it. You looked goofy, though. You wore a black hood and played chess with a knight.

"Now slow down there, cowpoke! That wasn't me."

Aren't you Death?

"If you see reason, I'll be *your* death. But not capital-D Death. Not Death, in general. I'm a specific sort of death. Think of me as an underling the capital-D guy delegates deaths to."

It talked about God, too.

"Ah, I see. So it was a fantasy film."

You just said that to get a stir out of me. Well, it's not going to work. The film was all about there basically not *being any such thing as God. I already know there's no such thing as God.*

"Of course you do. You're smarter than the average flesh-thing. So, just think: no God, no penalty for deciding your life's a mistake that you'd like to erase."

Maybe, just maybe, it isn't a mistake. Mr. Chin understands me in a way that other people don't. He's more... well... I guess you'd say... sophisticated. He doesn't grade things in a way that's all focused on right-or-wrong, black-or-white. He's willing to give credit for creativity. Like, this one time, he gave us this test with an essay question asking us to analyze this poem by Sylvia Plath, all about riding a horse at dawn. I hadn't read the damned thing. I wasn't about to pretend *that I'd read it. But I knew a little about it, because it had been discussed in class.*

So instead of writing an essay answer, I wrote a little story. I wrote a story about how this weird fungus planted itself in the pores of the horse's hide and how it grew and grew until it consumed the horse. By the end of the story, the horse was nothing but a galloping fungus, and the rider threw herself off the horse because she was all dainty and shit and the horse was too disgusting. She was also scared that if she didn't jump off, she would get the fungus, too. She broke her neck when she jumped off, but it was worth it. When I got the test back, I was expecting to get an F.

"But you didn't, did you, kiddo?"

No. He gave me an A+, "for imaginatively paraphrasing the theme". But I think he was worried he was going to get into trouble for doing that because right next to the grade, he wrote: "But tell no one."

"Heh... Now that's Larry Chin for you, a regular card. My

kinda guy. Never one to color inside the lines, that fellow. You get no bullshit from him. He doesn't care about all the shit your normal teachers care about. I mean, have you seen the way that guy dresses? He stretches the school's definition of casual, to be sure. Not the only boundary he stretches, either, if you catch my drift."

You make it sound like you know him.

Silence.

How do you know him?

Silence.

How do you know him?!

***

When you were fifteen, Mr. Suicide taunted you.

"He was your role model, kiddo. You said it yourself: you wanted to be *just like him*. Now's your chance. Go out into the garage at three in the morning and turn on the ignition. Then you'll be *just like him*."

You're an asshole.

"And *you're* out of reasons to stay alive."

You're forgetting something. I knew Mr. Chin. He was more than a teacher. He was my friend. I had him for Freshman Comp last year and World Literature this year. I don't think he killed himself. I think he was murdered.

"Oh, puh-lease! I know you're a kid, but you can't be that naïve. He was your friend, sure. Of course, if you think about it, no emotionally well-adjusted adult should *want* to be your friend, but I guess we now know that Eddie Chin wasn't emotionally well-adjusted, don't we? Not only do we know that he was your friend; we *also* know he was Andrea Matthews' lover. Her mother, for some crazy reason, objected. I suppose an age difference of twenty-seven years was a wee bit too much for her. Of course, without that little dalliance Mr. Chin would be without an heir. And then the whole world would be fighting over those cinder block and lumber bookshelves in his apartment and those '90s self-help paperbacks in his collection. Do you know he had one called *Care of the Soul*? Can you fucking believe it?"

Fuck. He knocked her up?

"I know. Careless, right? My understanding is Andrea's keeping the baby. I'm trying to talk her out of it. I keep whispering sweet nothings in her ear. I tell her that her life will be *practically* over, anyway, if she has that baby. I try to persuade her to go out like Ophelia, but she's hard-headed. Refuses to acknowledge my existence." Then Mr. Suicide giggled. "Hey, you know a thing or two about that, now. Don't you, kiddo? Girls refusing to acknowledge you exist, I mean." More giggles.

Maybe that's why he was murdered. Did you ever think about that? Andrea Matthews' dad wanted revenge, and so he killed Mr. Chin and made it look like a suicide.

"Here's another theory, Junior: Mr. Chin had read *Lolita* enough times to know a scholarly pedophile is a loathsome son of a bitch. He knew he couldn't help himself, and so he did the honorable thing. Or, hell, maybe he had no honor at all and just couldn't bear the idea of showing up on the six o'clock news. It's funny, you know. I have long talks with honorable and dishonorable people alike. Both give in to me, at times. You should be giving in to me. Your friend is dead, and you know you won't be getting another one."

That's bullshit. I'll have another friend before I leave high school. Fuck, I'll have a girlfriend before I leave high school.

"If you scrape the bottom of the barrel, maybe, kiddo. Because only the very bottom of the barrel is going to be interested in hanging out with *you.*"

    You can just fuck off! You hear me. Fuck. Off. You're not welcome here anymore. You're a fucking jackass. A fucking monster!

III

You lived on, mostly out of spite. Mr. Suicide was too obnoxious to give in to. In fact, you found Mr. Suicide too obnoxious to even *talk* to, right after that whole Mr. Chin ordeal. But, inevitably, the pressure didn't stop mounting. If anything, it got worse. You had to find another way—any other way—to deal with things.

So, in February of your sixteenth year, you turned to other, slightly less severe alternatives to suicide as a way to cope. At the gentler end of the spectrum, you considered playing hooky. At the more extreme end of the spectrum, you considered blinding yourself. One February morning you (sort of) combined the two.

You'd been assigned *Oedipus Rex* for a classical literature class. You hadn't read it. You half-paid attention to the class discussion. When you were called on, you took your head off of the desk just long enough to tell the teacher you hadn't read a word of it. "I'm not going to lie," you told her with self-defeating integrity, "I haven't even started it." There was no real reason for the other kids in the class to laugh, but they did. Like a movie audience chuckling at an unfunny joke, they did.

You hadn't replied to the teacher with malice, but she apparently thought you a little too nonchalant about it all. Or perhaps she thought your fellow students were laughing at her, instead of you. Maybe she felt threatened. You, alone, dared to not even *feign* attention. You hadn't even cheated in the manner that all the other kids cheated, by reciting details gleaned from a plot summary on Wikipedia. Perhaps, in the teacher's eyes, you were patient zero in a possible *epidemic* of apathy, and you needed to be neutralized immediately. She gave you a detention.

You honestly didn't care about staying after school for an hour (as much as you hated school, it was better than home). The only part that sucked was they called your mom that day to inform her of your infraction. When you got home, she said you weren't nearly as bright as what the school said you were. She made you sit down at the kitchen table and read *Oedipus Rex* right there while she browbeat you for a good hour and a half. Which were you supposed to do, read or listen to her? When you were reading, she seemed to hold it against you that you weren't listening to her. When you were listening to her, she seemed to hold it against you that you weren't reading.

When she noted you were cringing in sufficient humiliation, she took a deep breath, paused, and proceeded to call your father at work.

The first person your mother reached was a receptionist at the Ford plant. You could only hear little squeaks coming out of the land line receiver, but from your mother's responses (and your past experiences) you could infer that the receptionist was telling Mom that Dad was working on the line and he couldn't be pulled off unless it was an emergency. "But this *is* an emergency," Mom shrieked. When she was put on hold, she started yammering to you again. "See what your behavior's done? Making your father get pulled away from the assembly line? This is what you do to us. This is what you've always done to us."

You couldn't wait for Dad to get on the phone. At least then, her snark wouldn't be surging directly into you. But it turned out to be no more comfortable. If anything, it was even more uncomfortable for her to talk about you as though you weren't there. She loudly denounced you to him. She repeated the same criticism, over and over.

"He just got a detention," she said. "I'm not sure if any of our kids ever got detention. I mean, it's been a long time since we had a kid in high school, hasn't it? Maybe one of them got detention, somewhere along the way. But I don't think so. Anyway, something must be done. Ever since he hit middle school, he hasn't been the same boy. I think he's not as smart as the testing says he is. It was right at the end of elementary school that they gave him those tests and said he was super-smart. That's probably why he's not the same boy as he used to be. I'm going to talk to the school about it. Bright children do their assignments. I'm pretty sure if he could do the work, he would. I mean, you have your faults, that's for sure, but one of them isn't laziness. You've always been a good provider. And the good Lord knows I'm not lazy, either, doing all the work to keep the household going—all the work I have to do to keep *your son* focused on school. It's not easy being a mother, let me tell you. It's like you say: when you have kids, that's all you have.

"Anyway... like I said, it can't be laziness because he doesn't get that from either of us. So I can only assume it's above him. Those test scores were a fluke. Maybe even a mistake. Maybe there's another child with the same name, somewhere else in Louisville, and that child is the one who deserves all the opportunities your son is getting."

She talked to him for far too long. Minutes went by. Dozens of minutes went by. Your father would surely get chewed out by the foreman for gabbing on the phone with your mother that long. You would surely explode before she hung up the receiver. Once she built up a head of steam about something like this, she wouldn't stop talking until she'd exhausted herself. And, judging by the empty cup of coffee in front of her on the kitchen table, it would be a long time before she exhausted herself.

You looked up from *Oedipus Rex* and wanted to punch her. Surely, she had to know that her chatter was distracting you. She had you trapped in one of her patented no-win scenarios. Part of you thought that she'd sadistically planned it this way. If you earnestly tried to read the play, you would face constant frustration from the distraction. But if you stopped trying to read it, she would take that as all the more evidence it was beyond you.

You did the best you could to survive the ordeal. You flipped pages, but you didn't read. You skimmed. The pages were old and musty-smelling. Like maybe they'd been printed closer to Sophocles' time than yours. But you kept flipping them at a realistically slow pace.

It seemed like enough to satisfy your mother until she got off the phone. Then she looked at the clock. "Oh, dear, you've made me late for starting dinner." She frantically went to preheat the oven. (She always had dinner on the table at six o'clock, even though Dad frequently changed shifts. Dinner time could've just as easily changed along with his schedule. But she insisted it must never stray from six, and reacted with something close to rage if pressures forced a delay. Six o'clock was a time to which she'd assigned significant meaning. The fact that it was totally arbitrary didn't rein in her contempt. She let you know how rude you were to be messing it all up.)

She opened the refrigerator's freezer and grabbed a box of

fish sticks. Put them on a cookie sheet. When the oven beeped to announce it was at the right temperature, she slid them in. Then she started to get potatoes out to put in the microwave. Dinner presented a fresh crisis, and as you continued to try to read *Oedipus* she fidgeted back and forth—not really doing much *besides* fidgeting. Finally, she spoke to you. "What kind of son are you? You haven't even offered to set the table."

You knew how this was going to go. Really you did. Why did you even say the words? "Do you want me to get up from reading and help you, Mom? I can set the table for y—"

She yelled at you. "Don't you even pretend to be helpful, now! If a son really wanted to help his mother, he'd go ahead and start helping out without being asked. Now, go to your room!" With relief, you did as you were told. You thought that she might start to quiz you about *Oedipus Rex* over dinner, so you fired up your laptop and went onto Wikipedia to find a plot synopsis. You figured you should do this as soon as possible, because Mom would likely get the idea before too long that she should punish you by confiscating your laptop.

The summary of *Oedipus Rex* wasn't as simple as you'd wanted it to be. There was a lot of information jammed in there. The big take-away, though, was that Oedipus unknowingly slept with his mother and killed his father. Horrified by the revelations (and the suicide of his mother/wife), the dude blinded himself and begged to be exiled.

That's where you got the blinding idea. It wasn't that you were being dramatic and trying to be exactly like Oedipus. Your situations were totally different. You were no king, and you hadn't fucked *anyone* yet (let alone your mother). Nor had you killed anyone yet (although, yes, you'd had the urge). No, you were not Oedipus.

But that didn't mean you couldn't borrow Oedipus' answer.

Blinding, perhaps, offered some of the same comfort suicide did, but without quite so much fear attached. It would mean just losing your eyesight, not losing your existence. But, at the same time, it would offer some of the same features as losing your existence. You'd no longer have to look at all the ugliness. The ugliness in the mirror, the ugliness on your mother's face as she snarled and slapped you. The ugly grins of other kids at school when they were talking about you. Ugly, old teachers like Mr. Winnick. The ugliness of a city like Louisville; as gray and inconsequential as a ball of lint in a bum's pocket. It could all be gone, if you blinded yourself.

Even better, if you blinded yourself, you'd likely be re-moved—at least temporarily—from your parents' house. There'd be a hospital where you'd be taken away for treatment. Then they'd take you out of the regular kids' school and put you in the Kentucky School for the Blind. And, who knows, with a change of setting, you might even be able to transform yourself into something of a badass. You'd have several years of non-blind life under your belt, whereas some of the other students might have been blind from birth. You'd have the ad-vantage. You could be one of the cool kids at a blind school, couldn't you? Of course you could.

You turned off the lights in your room and put a pillow over your glasses to imagine what it would be like. It felt warm and cool and peaceful all at the same time. You couldn't relax, though. You couldn't relax because the walls were so thin you could hear the opening and shutting of various kitchen draw-ers as your mother prepared the meal. You knew it was only a matter of minutes until she would scream for you to come and get your food.

And that's just what happened. She screamed for you and she screamed for your brother-who-still-lived-at-home to come to the table. You knew that if you didn't hurry she wouldn't stop screaming. You went out to the table.

Your mother's tacky ceramic knickknacks rattled on the coffee table when you walked past them and into the kitchen. It wasn't that you were heavy. It's that the house had been made in a factory. It had been shipped out to the lot in two pieces and nailed together. Everything was made of plastic or the cheapest plywood. You'd been in trailers before. Your family had poor relations who lived in them. And that's exactly what it seemed like. It seemed more like a trailer than a house. But you knew better than to tell your mother that. She relished the relative affluence your father's union job at Ford granted her. It was a house, not a trailer. It was, to her, the farthest thing from a trailer in existence.

You sat at the table and saw the fish sticks sitting on a plastic plate your mother had gotten as a "collectible" from McDonald's sometime back in the '70s. There was half a baked potato next to them, and an unappetizing mush of green beans as the other side dish. You started to stab your fork and knife into the potato, when Mom slapped your hand. "Your brother's not out yet!" she said. "And after that, we say grace."

Your mother went back to your brother's door and knocked five times in rapid succession. "I *said*, it's dinner time!" You heard his door open and his footsteps follow Mom's out to the kitchen. She was like a prison guard or loony bin orderly coming to take her prisoner/patient to the cafeteria. All that was missing was a big mess of keys jangling on her hip.

When all three of you were finally seated at the dinner table, she asked your brother if he wanted to say grace. He didn't respond.

"Your brother's shy," she said. She sighed and folded her hands together. "I guess that means I'll have to do the honors.

Now let's all bow our heads. Father-God, we ask that you bless this bounty which you have provided us, and we thank you that we share meal time as a family. We thank you that we are not like so many other families these days, scattered all over the country, not even talking to each other each day. We thank you for the closeness we share. In the name of the Lord Jesus Christ. Amen."

From that point, it was like there was a race between you and your brother to determine which of you would finish and leave the table first. You wolfed down your fish sticks in two bites. The potato took longer because it was still hot. The beans could be mushed into a big gummy ball and shoveled in rather efficiently. Your brother finished in less than five minutes and then walked back to his room. You finished a minute or two after that.

You didn't want to spend any more time around your mother than you needed to, but you knew you'd be screwed if you didn't volunteer to help with dishes. When you asked, your mother laughed at you. Laughed, dramatically, like it wasn't a real laugh at all but forced. "You'll do anything to get out of reading that play, won't you? You'd even rather do dishes than be forced to increase your knowledge by trying something that's hard. I was born at night, but I wasn't born *last* night. I see though your tricks. Now I'm even more convinced that your classes are too hard for you. Go to your room. I don't want to see you the rest of the night."

You felt relieved. You liked your room, even if it wasn't much to look at. Like everything else in the house, it felt like a jail cell. But at least it felt like a semi-*private* jail cell. Sure, you could still hear the television in the living room blaring. But it gave you at least a *taste* of solitude and it contained everything in the world that was yours.

You put the pillow over your eyes again. You braced your-self for the noise of kitchen faucets gushing water; the noise of plastic McDonald's collectible plates clanking against each other. But you didn't hear them. Instead, you heard your mother let out a loud sigh, and you heard the television turn on. It was her favorite reality show—the one that had people dancing *and* singing *and* competing against one another. You heard her chuckle. You wondered if there was a way to make yourself deaf as well as blind.

You told yourself that you'd have to be practical. If you blinded yourself the way Oedipus did—if you stabbed your eyes with something sharp—there would be too much pain to do anything else. You wouldn't be able to move on to stab your eardrums, after that. You'd have to take one thing at a time. Which was more annoying? Sounds or sights?

For you, the answer was sights. If everything became black-ness, then there'd be no context for the noise. The noise wouldn't be coming out of anyone or anything, except the blackness. If you blinded yourself and then your mother spoke to you, you would laugh because it would seem to you like the blackness had come alive, and was imitating your mother like a comedian would. And oh, that would be a funny joke. That would be the funniest joke of all time.

There was an ice pick in one of the kitchen drawers. It hadn't been used in ages. Was there really any legitimate use for an ice pick? In the days before ice makers it may have had some utility but in the present day it seemed to only be useful as a weapon. Why did you even care about such things? You didn't care, really. You just thought it was odd. But then again, so many things about life were odd.

You decided you'd go ahead and blind yourself. You went out to the kitchen to get the necessary tool. You walked as quickly and quietly as you could. Your mother was absorbed in her show. There was no indication that she noticed you. If she did, she probably thought you were grabbing a pop. You put your hand on the drawer handle and gently pulled. It let out a little squeaking whine, but did so as a roar of applause poured out of the television. You picked up the ice pick, hid it in your pocket, walked off to your room, shut the door, and locked it.

Then you took off your glasses. Turned on the lights.

You stood there, in front of the mirror, weapon/tool/surgical instrument in hand. If you followed through, your life of inaction would come to an end. The rage and sadness you felt inside would finally have an escape valve. You'd have permanent scars to speak of your dissatisfaction with the world. Self-blinding offered more permanent relief than anything you'd tried before. More permanent than, say, masturbation (which worked, fleetingly, as a distraction and anxiety-reliever; but was insufficient for *continued* relief from the burdens of the world). You'd been thinking about how to find a way out for years. *This could be it.*

The wood of the ice pick handle was smooth in your hands. It felt good and it felt right. You picked it up with your left hand and put the tip of the ice pick up to your eye, so that the piercer and the piercee almost grazed one another. All you'd have to do is slam it into there. You wanted to do it. You told your arm and hand and fingers to comply with your request. But you felt a sudden aching. A tightness. The muscles, as though possessed of a will of their own, refused.

You were not ready, yet, to slam the ice pick into your pupil. It was there—waiting for you—just begging to be pierced. The black pupil against the brown iris seemed like a bull's eye inviting you to hit it. And it would be easy to hit. It wouldn't be like the time Dad had taken you clay target shooting at the outdoor range. You'd only hit one target that day (and that was unintentional… you'd pulled the trigger out of nervousness and gotten a target besides the one you were shooting for).

No, this target wasn't moving, nor was it thirty feet up in the air. The projectile wasn't birdshot. It was so simple, *so* simple. It would only take a second. You reckoned the pain would last far longer than that, but the *actual action* would only take a moment. Maybe not even a full second. Maybe a matter of milliseconds.

You should have been able to do it. You felt like you needed to do it.

But you weren't able to do it.

You threw yourself onto the bed and under the covers. Thrashed around in them. Let out little groans you hoped no one could hear. You wished, for a moment, you were in the loony bin. There, at least, you'd have rubber walls to bounce off of. Here, all you could do was fidget between sheets and regret that you lacked the courage of your convictions. You flicked a switch, and then the room was—for the most part— dark. But could still see a thin ray of light from a street lamp creeping into your room through a small gap in between your mini-blinds and the window. *Fuck the light*, you thought. You put the pillow back over your head, and that helped some. But it also made things feel stuffy. You couldn't do it for more than five minutes at a time. It got to be downright uncomfortable.

Of course, blinding yourself would be uncomfortable, too.

But that was different. It would be the discomfort that would end all discomfort. Just a bit of pain, you imagined, there for the first few months. They'd give you good drugs to lessen it. And then it would be gone and you'd have nothing but blessed blackness in its place. You wanted the blessed blackness. You needed the blessed blackness. But all you got, that night, was an eight-hour installment of blackness. And even *that* wasn't uncontaminated by vision. You had dreams. Terrible dreams of ugly faces in ugly places doing ugly things. You woke from them, crying and trembling. *What if I blind myself and still dream*, you thought. *Then all of it would be for nothing. The ugliness is everywhere. It's going to win. I can't escape it.*

***

You'd slept in your clothes. You didn't want to take a shower. You thought your mother was going to scold you for not having changed your clothes or showered, but when you walked out into the kitchen to grab some orange juice she didn't seem to notice. She greeted you in an unironically cordial manner.

"Why *there's* my baby boy," she said. She put her coffee down on the coaster and hugged you uncomfortably tight.

Your father was there, too. He was eating scrambled eggs that, from the smell, had been overcooked. "So," he said. "Detention, huh?"

You nodded.

"Your mother and I don't care for that."

You didn't want to have the conversation right then. It was tempting to have it then, because Mom seemed to be in one of her better moods. But you had to walk out to the bus stop, and you wanted to have some time alone there before all the other neighborhood kids came out. It was peaceful outside, at the bus stop, before all the other neighborhood kids came out. Quiet. Still.

"It won't happen again, Dad."

"He has to stay an hour afterward today," Mom said. "So the bus can't take him home. I'll have to leave and pick him up. That's going to make dinner late. It's really as much a punishment for the parents as it is a punishment for the kids."

"I'm sorry," you said. You weren't really sorry, but you knew if you didn't say it, you'd hear about it.

Your mother ignored what you said and babbled on. "I'm going to schedule a meeting with your teachers. I think we need to get you out of those gifted and talented classes and into something a bit less challenging. I think that's just the cure."

Your father finished chewing his eggs. "There are lots of good jobs out there for folks, even if they ain't gifted or talented. I mean, with the way your grades are going, I think we have to admit that—no matter what your test scores are—you're probably not going to college. But I'm going to start talking to HR about how we might be able to get you in over at the plant. You'd be making better money, out of high school, than a lot of kids will make coming out of college."

You didn't agree, but you nodded. *Another reason to blind myself,* you thought. *It would make me ineligible for factory work. Sure, I might still see ugliness in dreams, but at least I wouldn't have to end up like Dad.* This heightened your resolve.

Your mother insisted you eat some eggs before leaving for the bus stop. "You have plenty of time before the bus comes," she said. She piled a string of yellow and brown gunk on a plastic McDonald's collectible plate for you. You ate as quickly as you could. Then you went to your room and looked for the ice pick. At first you looked in your top drawer, but after that yielded nothing you remembered you'd fallen asleep with it in your hand. You looked in your bed. Found it in the midst of tangled sheets. You breathed a sigh of relief and plopped it into your backpack.

Your heart felt sick when you thought of how you hadn't been able to do the necessary deed, last night. But maybe the courage would arise this morning. Yes, that was always a possibility. Maybe the tension of school would be the incentive.

You had to go to the bathroom and take a piss. Standing over the toilet, you looked at various medicine bottles and household tonics. You saw a bottle of hydrogen peroxide, turned so that you could read its **DIRECTIONS** and **WARNINGS**. After you flushed the toilet, you read the label. "Do not use in eyes… In case of accidental ingestion, seek professional assistance, or contact a Poison Control Center immediately."

You grabbed it from the shelf. You didn't think anyone would notice it was gone. This could be an easier way of damaging your eyes. A chemical process, rather than a crude spike. All you'd have to do is allow the peroxide to make contact with the eyes. But how?

You grabbed a huge wad of toilet paper—twenty sheets long. Fortunately, the bathroom was across from your room. You were able to quickly sneak the bottle of hydrogen peroxide and the toilet paper into your room, without being spotted. The toilet paper squeezed into the backpack well enough, but you had too many books and folders in there for the peroxide to fit. So you removed all school-related material. Hid it all away in the back of your closet. Then you replaced it with the rest of the blinding supplies: the peroxide and the ice pick. You felt a wave of relaxation wash over you. No books, just blind: yes, *that* made you feel so much better. Then you remembered you'd also need the cotton belt off of your housecoat. You tossed it in, too.

Your plan was this: you would—at some point in the school day—sneak away to an empty room or stairwell where you would blind yourself using the ice pick. If you couldn't summon up the will to do that, the hydrogen peroxide was your Plan B. The label said not to get it into your eyes. So if you intentionally forced it into your eyes, well, that would surely cause some damage, now, wouldn't it? Would it blind you? You weren't sure. But it would have to do some damage. And if you *repeatedly* forced the hydrogen peroxide into your eyes, over long stretches of time, then that had to inflict some *significant* damage.

If you lacked the courage to use the ice pick, you'd dab some of the hydrogen peroxide on a piece of toilet paper. Then you'd force your eyes wide open and stick the wad of peroxide-soaked toilet paper right on top of one. Kind of the same way you'd seen people put contact lenses in. You'd do that to one eye, and then you'd do it to another. Finally, you'd tie the housecoat belt around your eyes, to hold the toilet paper in.

Yes, that's exactly what you would do. You hoped it would burn your eyes and render them no longer functional. At the very least, you hoped it would hurt. You hoped it would punish your eyes for seeing so much ugliness.

With all your tools for self-injury packed away, you marched out to the living room. Mom's coffee table knickknacks clattered and shook once again, under your steps. You told her you were going now. She sipped coffee and waved goodbye to you. Dad waved, too. Waved a little too excitedly, like someone waving bon voyage to a cruise ship.

When you escaped out the front door, you saw your breath in the air. You should have picked up some gloves. You should have worn a coat. You didn't like the idea of going back in and having to say "goodbye" all over again, but you did. You put on your coat and your gloves.

"There he is, the absent-minded professor!" your mother said.

In your coat pocket, you flipped her the bird.

You walked back out and felt the weight of the household fall from you. It felt good, for a moment. Then you realized you got out later than you'd wanted to. You jogged off your front porch and down the stairs. Over the years, they had begun to work themselves away from the foundation, so that when you stepped on them, they tilted. This made you trip, but you righted yourself before falling.

There were already other kids at the bus stop. The minute they spotted you walking toward them, they started laughing.

"We need to stop calling him Trash Ass," one of them said. You were surprised, because you didn't expect the least bit of sympathy from this crowd. The dude—a senior, no less—looked at you. "You'd like that, wouldn't you?"

You looked at the ground and nodded back.

"We need to stop calling him that," the senior said, "because it's not just his ass that smells like trash!" He smiled. "I can smell his b.o. from here. Let's call him Trash Pits!"

The other kids started laughing. "Trash Pits! Trash Zits," they chanted, nonsensically.

You couldn't bear it any longer. You were not one of them. It was high time that you stopped going through the motions of being one of them. You walked away from the bus stop.

"Awww," the senior said, "we hurt his widdle feewings."

"H-he's really leaving... " a girl said. She giggled, then repeated herself. (This time, sounding incredulous rather than mocking.) "Oh wow... he's *really* leaving."

You kept walking. Out of your little white trash subdivision. Onto the sidewalk. Into your neighborhood, a suburban area called Hikes Point. Not the poorest place in Louisville. Not the richest.

You didn't have any idea where you were going. You just knew you weren't going to school.

Where you going, Trash-Pits, to deposit yourself in the dump?

Honestly, that didn't sound half bad. But you knew of a little city park, an odd wooded area nestled in the suburbs. It was only about five blocks away. You decided you'd go there and do what you'd planned to do. It made a hell of a lot more sense than trying it at school, anyway.

It felt freeing to play hooky. (Even if your plans were to just spend all day outside, in the cold.) The park had a soccer field, but you ignored that and walked onto the nature trail, instead. It had been three whole weeks since the last snow. But there, in the shade provided by the trees, there were little remnants that lingered. Snow trapped in an oak's bark and in its roots. Snow crusted over fallen leaves.

You went off the trail, to the darkest, most densely forested area you could find. It was white with snow and brown with leaves and black with shadows. You lay down there. You used the backpack as a pillow, and you breathed.

It wasn't true wilderness. You still heard cars zoom by. You still heard airplanes overhead. In fact, you'd not been there too long when you even heard someone else tramping through the trail. They didn't seem to stumble on to you, though. That, at least, made you feel relieved.

After you had rested for about fifteen minutes, you fetched the ice pick out of your bag. Then you realized you hadn't brought a mirror. But you could aim without a mirror, couldn't you? It wasn't *that* hard.

That's when it dawned on you. You would never blind yourself, for the same reason you would probably never kill yourself. You were a gutless coward. What were you doing out there? When your mother found out you not only skipped detention, but skipped school altogether, she would rage at you. You should try to scurry back. You should beg for forgiveness. If you hurried back and came up with some excuse for missing the bus, you might be able to set everything right.

You endeavored to get up off your ass and do all that. You really, really wanted to do all that. But once again, your muscles wouldn't follow your brain's directions. So you lay there, in the cold. When your muscles sufficiently un-froze, you got up on your knees and opened up your backpack. You had to snort snot back into your nose. You had to wipe a lingering thread of it off with your jacket sleeve.

You got out the peroxide, the toilet paper, and the housecoat belt. And then, you executed Plan B. Wadded up some toilet paper like a cotton ball. Put the toilet paper up to the mouth of the peroxide bottle. Turned the bottle upside down to soak the toilet paper through. Repeated those steps with a second wad of toilet paper. You took off your glasses, then pried your eyelid wide open with your right hand while you put the peroxide-soaked t.p. onto the eyeball, itself, with the left.

The peroxide felt so cold against the skin adjacent to the eye. Felt cold on the eye itself, too. It felt cold, and it stung. Stung so fiercely that, at first, you winced and shuddered. But in a matter of moments, you learned to love it. The stinging was like life embracing you. For the first time in a long time, embracing you. You felt something. And if you felt, you counted. You existed. It took you momentarily out of the pain in your head and the pain in your heart and reminded you that you really existed as something material. You weren't merely a disembodied spirit. "You're solid," the pain insisted. "You're real".

You groped for the housecoat belt. Tied it tight around your head in such a manner that it kept the toilet paper in constant contact with the eyeball. Then you pulled it up a little so you could see out of your other eye. So you could hurt it in the same way. And when you did, when the pain embraced both of them, simultaneously, you felt yourself getting a hard-on. You unzipped your pants. Wriggled your jeans and underwear down to your knees. Life was no longer merely embracing you. It was stroking you. You stroked back, whimpered, and came. Wiped your hand off on the cold earth beside you.

Afterward, there was more desolation. Wind blowing through leafless branches. The sound of critters hopping around you. Woodpeckers at work. The traffic along the main drag quieting as rush hour wound down and the day progressed toward mid-morning. There was even a moment of relief from noise, entirely. Just one moment. You held onto it as long as you could, savored it, because you knew it wasn't going to last long.

This was hooky. The only day *during your entire high school career* that you played hooky. After a stretch of time that might have been one hour or six, you took off your blindfold, removed the peroxide-soaked toilet paper, put your glasses back on, and assessed your vision. Unfortunately, you still saw things. As far as you could tell, there'd been no damage, at all, to your eyesight. For a moment, your eyes felt itchy, but even that didn't last long. You couldn't tell what time it was, but you suspected that, by now, your absence from school would be noted.

Right on cue, text messages started to arrive. First from the school and then, only seconds later, from your mother. You only read enough of them to notice who they were from. You knew that there could be nothing valuable gained from actually reading them.

You dismissed the messages, but they were soon replaced by new ones. The phone blurped and beeped and buzzed to announce them. You used the ice pick to clear away any lingering snow from the ground. Then you used it to dig. The ground was not frozen. The earth was rich and black and wet. You dug a grave about six inches deep, six inches long, and six inches wide for your cell phone. It kept on protesting, blurping and beeping and buzzing as you buried it.

You whispered to it. "Don't go into the grave fighting. Accept it. I'm killing you."

It blurped. It beeped. It buzzed.

You tossed the cold wet earth back on top of it.

It blurped. It beeped. It buzzed. *Even after you'd fully buried it*, it blurped and beeped and buzzed. That was the most hilarious thing of all. The fact that, even after it had been committed to the earth, it still insisted you needed to acknowledge its importance. You giggled, then tried to get more rest. But the muffled phone-chirps distracted you from rest. You momentarily considered digging it up, if for no other reason than to remove the battery and rebury it. But you decided, instead, to move on.

You had to pull your underwear back on. Pull your pants back up. When finished, you stood up and found a muscular man with a blond buzz cut and mustache staring at you. He wore a black leather jacket, gray T-shirt, jeans, and leather boots. He looked much older. Like, maybe in his thirties.

"I saw that sexy little show you put on," he said. "Blindfolds. Kinky stuff. You've got my interest. "

You'd been spotted. You'd been spotted and horribly misunderstood. "It wasn't what it looked like. What I mean is, I'm not like that."

The man grinned. "Of course you aren't." He stepped toward you. Extended his hand to shake. Looking closely, you noticed it was slathered with semen. "My name's Andrew," he said. "What's yours?"

"I have to go now."

"You look like a good submissive boy. Come now, come to Daddy and lap up your cum like a good little lad now." He talked to you like he would a puppy. "Come on now. Come, boy."

The bottle of peroxide, some stray strands of toilet paper, the ice pick, and your backpack were all still on the ground where you'd left them. You had a weapon, with the ice pick. You lurched quickly backwards and grabbed it. Brandished it. You didn't want to kill him. You just wanted to get out of there.

"So it's like that, then," he said.

"Yeah," you said. "It's like that then." You left everything besides the ice pick behind. You kept *it* close to your body. Decided it was best wielded as a defensive weapon. Andrew eyed you, warily.

You felt you were finally safe, but you weren't. The moment you slipped past him and turned your back to run like hell away from there, he grabbed you.

"If you're gonna go ahead and tease my cock like that," he said, "then turnabout's fair play. I'm gonna tease *yours*, too." He slapped your ass, almost like he was spanking it. Then he reached between your legs and, through your jeans, stroked your still semi-hard cock.

You felt disgusted at yourself when it responded with a twinge. You felt disgusted at him when you realized the cum that had been on his hands was now on your jeans. You ran. He held on and for a few harrowing seconds it looked like he was going to prevail. Like his muscles and bulk were going to drag you to the ground. You turned around far enough to plant the ice pick in his shoulder. You saw something red pop in the air, like a liquid firecracker. He winced and wailed and cursed.

You were not the strongest kid in high school. You were no football player or wrestler. But adrenaline infused your muscles with strength and, more importantly, with will. Your assailant fell to his knees. You ran out of the park and—because you hadn't anyplace else to go—back home.

As you did so, you realized you should have felt grateful for escaping the ordeal. You should have been thankful you'd had the ice pick with you. But your mind wasn't focused on gratitude. Instead, it was focused on self-blame. Why, oh, why had you not exerted the same degree of strength, the same amount of will, to use it to pluck out your eyes?

IV

Mom slapped you the moment you walked in the door. She must have been waiting there to ambush you. That's the only way she could've been able to pull that off. You didn't even see it coming. "Bastard! How do you think this makes our family look?!" she screamed. Then she threw one of the knickknacks at you. It missed far to the right.

You told her you had to use the bathroom. You didn't want to have this discussion with Andrew's partially-dried-up cum on the butt and crotch of your jeans. She hadn't noticed it yet. But in time, she would, and you didn't want to have that conversation. Mom ran after you, tried to stop you from reaching the bathroom, but you got there half a second before her. Locked the door. She pounded.

"You can't run away from me! You can't run away from your problems, either! Your father's heartbroken about this. He volunteered to go into work early today, and I had to call him off the line to tell him about this. Do you know what that does to him, when he gets called off the line? Do you?" Her voice cracked midway through that last question.

You ran the water and took a washcloth to your jeans. Scrubbed them until the stains were off.

"Do you know what that does to him?" your mother screamed through the door. "Do you know what it does to his position at work when he has to constantly get called off the line?"

"Then *don't call him off the fucking line!*" You were so done with playing her game.

She growled. She screamed. "What did you say to me?!"

After you'd made your jeans presentable, you threw the washcloth in the hamper. Wiped your nose on your jacket sleeve. Cleared your throat.

"I said, *don't call him off the fucking line!* Fuckin' bitch… don't you get it? The things you call him about, the things you call 'emergencies'… they aren't emergencies at all. *At all.* You need to give Dad a break. You know that's why he volunteers for all those extra shifts, don't you?"

"What are you talking about? This discussion isn't about any of that. This discussion is about…"

"He works all those extra shifts because he can't fucking stand you. He. Can't. Fucking. Stand. You!"

The next round of screaming made you flinch. Made you sick to your stomach and dizzy. You couldn't even hear what she was saying. She was screaming and she was ramming her shoulder into the door. It was a cheap door made of cheap wood and mounted on cheap hinges. After she'd rammed it ten times, it came loose. Fell toward you. Nailed you on the head. Disoriented you enough that she had time to plow her way into the bathroom, shove the fallen door to the side, and nail you again with a series of slaps on the face. "Disgrace. You're a fucking disgrace to this family," she said, as she wailed on you.

You reared back and punched her. Showed no restraint. Let her have it. She'd been needing a good whoopin' for sixteen years. Your first blows landed on her stomach. And when she was momentarily disabled, bent over, you rammed your knee into her nose. You heard a crack and (for the second time that day) saw a spray of red. You made a sound halfway in between a groan and a laugh. When she stopped fighting back, you stopped, too. Whoopin' her exhausted you. You slumped onto the toilet.

"Don't you ever scream at me again," you said. "From here on out, things are going to be different. Do you understand me?"

Blood from your mother's smashed nose dripped onto her upper lip, and from there onto her teeth. She was confused. Mumbling something. Something soft. Her lower lip quivered like that of a frightened toddler.

"Louder, bitch. Answer me when I talk to you. I said, *did you hear me?*"

A voice answered, but it wasn't your mother's. "Y-you're in t-trouble."

It was older-brother-who-never-left-home. He had his cell phone in his hand. "I've called the police. They're coming to stop you from killing Mom."

You sighed. You were about to go ahead and hit him, too, for being so fucking stupid. But you figured that wouldn't look good when the cops arrived. So you took a deep breath and tried to calm your brother down. "Now look... you need to call them back. Tell them that it was all a big mistake. Look, I didn't *kill* her."

"You were trying to," he said. "You were trying to kill our mother."

"Look, she attacked me. I was just fighting back."

He glared at you. "I *know* you've wanted to kill her."

And he probably *did* know that you'd wanted to kill her, because *he'd* probably wanted to kill her at one point, too, before he'd surrendered to her control.

"I've never wanted to kill her," you lied. "And don't you dare tell the cops that I did."

Your mother was now coherent, but sounded awkward. Sounded like she had a bad head cold. She had to breathe with her mouth open, because when she tried to breathe through her nose, little bubbles of red-tinged snot formed and popped. "No police," she said. Then she started weeping, and babbled through the tears. "W-we're not the kind of family that calls police. We're not going to be the kind of family where one of our little boys is taken away from home and locked in jail. We're not."

Your brother started pacing the hallway, running his fingers through his hair. He was talking to himself. "If I do as she says, then it could happen again. And what if she dies? What if she dies? What if she dies? What if she dies?"

You started to clean things up. There were splinters of wood on the ground. You threw the biggest in the trash. You leaned the broken door against the wall outside the bathroom. You washed your hands to get your mother's blood off of them. You got a fresh wash cloth and started to clean up her face, but she slapped your hand when you tried. "I'm not a baby," she said.

"Oh yeah? You're crying like one."

"You little faggot! How dare you, you little faggot. Guess who's going to be crying as soon as the police leave this house. Guess who's going to be crying then, faggot?"

You wanted to belt her again, but couldn't. Made a fist. Gritted your teeth.

Then, the knock on the door. Your brother opened it.

The cop had one of those deep-southern voices, more Nashville than Louisville. Young guy. Not much older than you. "Are you the man who called?" he asked your brother.

"Yes. They're in the bathroom. Mom's hurt."

Only because she deserved *to hurt*, you thought.

The cop didn't react much at all, when he walked past the broken door in the hallway. Didn't react much at all when he saw Mom and you in the bathroom. He must have seen this sort of thing all the fucking time.

"Okay, you… the mother… I'm going to be taking a statement from you first." He got a notepad and pen out of his shirt pocket.

"N-no statements," she said.

"I'm afraid that since I've been called out here, ma'am, there's going to have to be a statement."

"No charges," she said.

He sighed. Put his notepad back in his pocket. "I understand you don't want any charges filed. But it looks like your nose is broke. I think you're going to need to go to the hospital. I'll call an ambulance."

"No ambulances," she said. "And, officer, I'd like for you to leave."

"You need medical attention."

"I'll drive her," your brother said. "I'm so sorry I called. I didn't mean it, Mom, honest I didn't. I didn't want to do something you didn't want me to, but I was nervous, you know? Pretty nervous, I mean. You know? I can drive her. I have a driver's license. I run errands for the family, all the time. I can drive her."

The cop nodded. "Okay, so if I leave here, I have your assurance you'll drive her to the hospital."

"Urgent care," Mom said. "No hospitals."

The cop sighed again. "Okay, fine. Urgent care."

Then he looked at you. "Okay now, sport, let's you and I take a walk outside and get some things straight."

What choice did you have? You went.

"What's up with your eyes," the cop said. "You been smoking pot?"

"I'm not high. You can drug test me right here and now."

"Then why are they all red?"

You couldn't tell him about the peroxide, so you told a lie. "There's pinkeye going around school. I think I might have it."

The cop backed up a step, but kept yammering. "You know somethin', sport, I don't think I believe you. I think you got all goofy on weed and maybe a hundred other things and started wailing on your mother for no good reason. That's what I'm thinking: you intimidated her into not pressing charges. Hell, I might-could arrest you anyway, *even if* she won't press charges, just to put a little inconvenience in your day. Empty out your pockets."

What could you do? You complied. There was nothing in there that would incriminate you.

"Back pockets, too."

You did as you were told.

"Now your jacket pockets."

You obeyed.

He looked at you. Craned his head. Stared into your eyes. Shook his head. "*On what planet* do you think it's acceptable to behave that way? To hit a woman. Not just any woman. Your own fucking mother!"

You didn't say anything. You wanted to tell him that she'd started it, but you already knew he wouldn't believe you. So you didn't mention it.

"Now, speak up! I asked a question. Always answer a police officer when he asks you a question."

"What was your question?"

"I'll repeat myself once, and that's it. I asked you: *on what planet do you think it's acceptable to behave that way?*"

"I-I don't know."

The cop mimicked you. Sashayed his hips and lisped dramatically when he mimicked you. "I don't know?"

Oh, fuck, how you wanted to steal that guy's pistol and unload it in his face.

"Well," the cop said, "the reason you probably don't know is that *there is no planet* in the universe where it's acceptable to behave that way. So, then the next question is: why do you behave so unacceptably? And do *not* tell me you have a chemical imbalance. Jesus Christ, if I hear another teenager say they're bipolar-schizophrenic this week, I'm going to go bipolar-schizophrenic, myself."

You knew that you were being lectured, and that there was no way for you to get out of it. The cop, not so long out of high school himself, was another in the line of bullies you'd faced in your life. You knew that this variety of hazing, like all the other varieties, wouldn't be done until he said it was done. You knew that, like all bullies, the cop wanted you to go along with it. He wanted you to not even resist. So you just went along with it. You didn't even resist.

"There's no reason for me to behave so unacceptably," you said.

"That's right," the cop said, "there isn't. Now, you're learning. You see... if I wanted to, I could take you into custody right this minute because what you said right there is pretty much a confession. But your mom said that she didn't want to press charges, and my boss gets all pissy if we give the commonwealth attorney's office a lot of cases that don't pan out. But remember that, if I had a bad day and didn't give a shit what my boss thought, I'd haul you in right now. Do we understand each other?"

You nodded. "Yeah, I understand you, officer."

"Good boy," he said. "Now, I'm going to get out of here. I better not get called out here again. Is that understood?"

"Yes, officer."

You read the name tag on his shirt. D. Collins. Officer Douchebag Collins, you decided his name was. You didn't want to run afoul of that guy ever again.

Later, though (*much* later) you did. But there's more stuff to explain before you can talk about that part.

V

Because you'd skipped detention and were discovered to have played hooky, the school suspended you. It was a crock. Part of some new so-called zero tolerance policy in regard to truancy. Three days without classes shouldn't have been such a bad thing, but your mother made them miserable.

"I can't take away your laptop," she confessed, "because the school wants you to do work online while you're here at home, and you damn well aren't using mine for that. But I can take away your cell phone. There's no reason for you to have one, until you go back to school."

You didn't have the courage to tell her that, by now, it was dead. Dead and, literally, buried.

"I lost it," you said. "It was in my backpack. I lost them both."

"Again! This is the third phone we've gotten you since you were twelve, and you lose every single one." She crossed her arms. Gritted her teeth. "And that backpack, too? I don't believe you. This is a trick, to hide your phone from me so I can't take it away. To hide your backpack from me so I can't search it for drugs!"

You had to make up a story. Something she'd find believable. "I think I lost them over by the bus stop. I put them down, one day, I don't even remember when, and then—just like that—they were gone. I looked and looked, but wasn't able to find them. I think maybe one of the other kids took them."

Her face turned red. "Lies! That's the same thing you said the last time you 'lost' your phone. You sold it, didn't you. Sold it for drugs. That's it. It makes sense, now. You're on drugs! You traded your phone for them, didn't you? Well, you won't be getting another phone from your father and me! We aren't going to aid and abet you in your filthy habits!"

You told her you'd swear on the Bible that you'd never taken drugs. You told her you didn't care at all about not having a cell phone. Told her that, in fact, you preferred it.

She demanded you empty your pockets. She searched your coat. Then she searched your room, looked through your underwear drawer. Your desk drawers. In your pillow cases. Under your bed. She even went so far as to remove books from your book shelf, thinking that you might have hidden the phone (or the drugs you'd allegedly purchased *with* your phone) in between two paperbacks.

While she was at it, she also *confiscated* a couple of paperbacks—your *The Catcher in the Rye* and an old Harry Potter book. It was as though she wasn't going to be happy unless she found *something* to take away from you, and fell back on religious objections to justify it.

She pointed at *Catcher*. "The Christian Parents Network has a warning about this one. It teaches disobedience," she said. "Disobedience and vulgarity and blasphemy!" Then she pointed at *Harry Potter*. "Witchcraft! The demonic, dressed up all nice and handsome like a decent young man, but *not* a decent young man. No, not at all."

You wanted to go ahead and belt her again. That would at least shut her up. But you didn't want to have another conversation with Officer Douchebag Collins (or any other officer, for that matter). Besides, if this was what she needed to focus on to get her mind off your cell phone, so be it. There was something to be said for picking your battles. Instead of giving her a good clobbering over this, you decided to let her have the illusion of victory. That way, she'd shut up about the cell phone and eventually leave.

She sat on the floor, ripping the brown and yellow cover off of *Catcher*. Grinning. Sweating. There was a sick glee she exuded as she destroyed something she thought you held dear. It wasn't a big deal, though. You'd gotten the book at a school library sale. Spent all of fifty cents on it. Hadn't even read it, yet, because whenever you tried reading *any* book these days you couldn't concentrate. So you didn't say a word about it. Just let her do her thing.

Same with Harry Fucking Potter (who found himself literally trampled under your mother's foot, then heaved—all gazillion pages of him—against the wall with a thud).

"If he's a warlock, then you probably should burn him," you said. "Instead of wrestling with him."

She sneered and picked the Harry Potter book up off the floor. Took it with her into the living room. "The book's getting tossed into the trash. It's *the author*, and all those who read her, who will be cast in fire on Judgment Day. And if you don't believe me, bear in mind, *I'm* not the one who says that, *God* does."

And with that, she went off to the kitchen and dumped the shredded remains of *Catcher* and the trodden corpse of *Harry Potter* in the trash can. You then heard her turn on the TV. She started chuckling at Drew Carey on *The Price is Right*.

***

You hurried through your online school work as quickly as you could, not really caring about getting the answers right. You finished the assignments in the afternoon of the first day of your suspension. You just wanted to get them finished so that you could say that you'd completed them. Afterward, you crawled in bed and put the cool, refreshing pillow over your face.

The next two days you stayed in your room, in bed, but pretended to still be at work on the assignments. On those days, your mother seemed far less interested in you than she'd been before. Overnight, she'd become withdrawn—absorbed into some deep, dynamic thought process to which you weren't privy.

When you ventured out to the kitchen for lunch, she didn't say a word to you. She was crocheting, and so absorbed in it that she didn't even seem to notice you were in the same room with her.

Later that afternoon, when you went out to grab a pop from the fridge, she was in the living room reading the Bible while Jerry Springer blared on the TV. She sat in her rocking recliner. She was rocking over and over. Looking at her more closely, she appeared to not have slept the night before. Her hair was frizzy and tangled. Her eyes were bloodshot and had dark shadows under them. She should have been reclining, not rocking.

She didn't even have dinner on the table at six. You didn't mind, though. Neither did your brother. You both fixed yourself some cereal. You both seemed relieved to not have to go through the motions of a Happy Family Dinner. You offered to make your mother a bowl of cereal. She muttered something about not being hungry, and then kept reading her Bible. When you'd been out there earlier, she was at the very start of it. Apparently in Genesis. Now, she was leafing through the end of the volume's onionskin pages. Revelation. Obviously she'd been skimming, not reading.

She had a savage, sexual expression on her face. You jerked your glance away from her when you realized the expression wasn't just an expression. The Bible sat on her lap. As her left hand flipped pages, she tucked her right hand in her crotch. She was bucking her hips against it. Grunting. Panting. The recliner squeaked with each motion.

You went back to your room and tried to forget you'd seen what you'd seen. Tried erasing the mental image from your mind. But you couldn't.

***

The worst part of returning to school was finding out your grades on the assignments you'd completed online, while suspended. They, predictably, ranged from average to poor. They didn't help your cause any.

Mom followed through on her promise to have you removed from gifted and talented classes. There was a meeting between her and some teachers, just to make it all official. When you returned from suspension, you were in classes with not-quite-smart, not-quite-dumb kids. Some of the classes used books you'd used the previous year.

In theory this could've been a chance to have a clean slate. Make new friends. That sort of thing. But the medium-level kids pretty much hated you on sight. They sized you up easily. They knew something your mother and the teachers didn't: you weren't one of them.

The homework was easier, but you still didn't bother doing it. After all, it wasn't the degree of difficulty that had prevented you from doing your homework in the more advanced classes. It was that you didn't care. If anything, you cared even *less* about school after your demotion.

You spent a lot of time in your room, and Mom didn't pester you much about that. Right after you'd punched her, you'd told her that things were going to be different, from then on out. You didn't really believe it yourself, when you'd said it. But the awesome thing was: you were right, sort of. After the initial tongue-lashing from Dad and the two or three evenings Mom cried and put you on a guilt trip about her medical bills, it was all over.

Your mother didn't want to admit to herself that what had happened, happened. Dad had to replace the bathroom door and that made him grumpy, but when all was said and done he took his cues from Mom. After two or three days, things were almost back to normal. No more tongue-lashings. No more guilt trips.

In some ways, breaking your mother's nose was the best thing you'd ever done. You felt less angry in the days afterward, like the violence had released a lot of pent-up anger.

You wondered about Andrew-from-the-park. You were pretty sure he wasn't going to press charges either (or for that matter, even contact the cops). Sure, you hurt him, but—just like with Mom—you only hurt him because you *had* to.

In any event, given what he was up to at the time, the cops were probably the last people that dude wanted to talk to. But still, you never knew, did you? He could always claim he was minding his own business when he was attacked by an un-kempt youth. Your backpack was still at the scene of the crime. (As was your peroxide.)

You had nothing in the backpack that would lead people to know it was yours, though. No school assignments, no identifying information of any sort. So, at least there was that. It would be a puzzling sight for a stranger to run across—your backpack with a bottle of peroxide just sitting there in a wooded area, a few clumps of soggy toilet paper nearby. Maybe your possessions would stay there forever. It was a secluded area. Maybe no one would ever discover them, not even for years. That idea appealed to you. You thought you'd maybe even go back there, someday, and think about those few moments of bliss you'd enjoyed, when things were quiet and your eyes were soaked in the blessed blackness.

VI

In the summer after your junior year, you spent a lot of time in your room with the pillow over your eyes. Your mother didn't replace the peroxide bottle that you'd left at the park. She didn't even notice it was missing. You still wanted the darkness, but you'd abandoned your only tools to obtain it. You couldn't even go walk to the park to retrieve them. She had you on a tight leash.

She'd never consented for you to take driver's ed. Said you were too nervous to handle it, that you'd accidentally kill yourself in a wreck.

She didn't allow you to get a summer job, either. She said that your grades proved you couldn't handle such responsibilities. She said she needed you to help clean the house. She told you to scrub out the bathtub twice a week.

You did those things. You thought, once again, about killing her. Mr. Suicide came back, as well, to remind you that he was an option. "Your brother still lives here, remember that," he said. "There's no getting out. She has control and she isn't about to lose it."

I turn eighteen next April, you reminded him. *I can gut it out until I get out.*

"You're one tough son of a bitch (no pun intended)," Mr.

Suicide said. "But the line between bein' a tough son of a bitch and a *crazy* son of a bitch is pretty damned gray. I think you're fixin' to cross over it, if I do say so, myself. Like your brother before you."

I'll never be like my brother!

Mr. Suicide started to giggle. "I wonder if his ears are burning. Or, better than that, I wonder if he can hear me. As you so often lament, the walls *are* quite thin. And you may have already guessed that I've spoken to other members of your family, too. Maybe he hears me through the wall and recognizes my voice. You're not my only prospect here. Sadly, not even the most *promising* prospect here. Every time I start to think you and I are ready to close the deal, you go off and get some brief *attachment* to someone, or you get all candy-ass on me and opt for self-mutilation, instead. Good thing there are other people here in this house who listen to what I have to say. Good thing I don't have to go out of my way to visit you. Because if I did, I might write you off as hopeless."

I don't want my brother to kill himself.

Mr. Suicide mocked you, taking on a faggoty tone as he mimicked you. "I don't want my bwutha to kill himsewlf," he whined. "When did *you* become Mr. Compassionate? And, hey, who said I was talking about your brother? There are two other people under this roof, you know?"

I don't want anyone else in this house to kill themselves.

"That's a lie," Mr. Suicide said. "You wouldn't bat an eyelash if a certain M-O-M did herself in."

You're trying to throw me off the trail. I know better than to think she'd kill herself. She's too happy making all of us miserable to want to kill herself. She doesn't even think about stuff like that. You're talking to my brother, aren't you?

No answer.

Aren't you?

"I'm under no obligation to go into details."

Look, why do you have to drag all of my family into this? I thought this was just between you and me.

"No man is an island," Mr. Suicide said. "You're all connected by your foul genetics. You are all merely tributaries of the same polluted river, and that river is called Insanity. There is no way to avoid it. It's your destiny to go mad. Or perhaps another metaphor will better explain it: insanity is the highway on which you're traveling. *I'm* the only off-ramp."

You told Mr. Suicide, once again, to fuck off. And the voice (yes, now you were certain, an audible *voice*... not your own thoughts) did as it was told. But did he simply move to another room of the house? Maybe pass through the wall to torment your brother? You didn't want that. You couldn't really say that you loved him. He'd called the cops on you, after all, and you were still plenty pissed off about that. But you didn't wish him ill.

So you were greatly relieved when, mere moments after Mr. Suicide left, there was an unfamiliar knock on the door. Not the five quick knocks that were your mother's signature. No, only two knocks that were barely knocks. Knocks that sounded more like fingernails scraping the door than actual knocks. You rolled off the bed and shuffled toward the door. Opened it. It was your brother. He looked back and forth, as though trying to make certain no one was watching. He had a manilla envelope in his hand. "Let me in," he whispered, "before she sees us."

You did as he asked.

The two of you spoke in hushed tones. Not exactly in whispers but not in a normal tone of voice, either.

"I heard him," your brother said. "I heard him talking to

you. I thought he was going to get you, but it looks like you told him what's what, huh? I mean, you know… he's not going to convince you to kill yourself."

You felt a tightness, a pinching in your stomach. You felt yourself shrinking away from him, the way you would from a dead bird or a pile of dog shit. Your disgust was not quite rational (after all, you'd already admitted to yourself Mr. Suicide was real). And yet, rational or not, you felt it.

Your reaction didn't escape your brother's notice. "The walls are thin," he reminded you (as if you needed any reminding). "And I'm right next door, so of course I'm going to hear things."

"Can Mom and Dad hear him, too?"

"I think they do, but pretend they don't. They're good at that, you know? Pretending things aren't happening, I mean. You know… like… not to make you feel bad, but when you beat up Mom, she pretended like it didn't really happen. You know, like how we never talk about it any more, and it's almost like things are back to normal. Like it never really happened. She's good at that, you know. Pretending, I mean. Pretending that things don't really happen."

You thought back to the day he first went mad. The thrashing. The sobbing. The way Mom and Dad just sat there instead of getting him help. The way you knew no one in that house would ever get help. He was mad, and even *he* knew that your mother ignored things she had no right to ignore. You might well be going mad, and even *you* knew it. *So maybe they overhear the voice, but pretend it's only the television,* you thought. And that made perfect sense to you.

"I couldn't make out all the words," your brother said, "but I could make out his tone, you know? He's a sarcastic p-pain in the ass."

You figured this meant that Mr. Suicide had targeted your

brother, before you. (How else would he know the voice?) You asked, "So, he's tried to convince you, too?"

"Yeah, but... but I found; well... how do I?... what I mean is... I found some salvation... I'm not g-gonna kill myself because the ugliness isn't as awful as I thought. See, here's the thing... my guess is that you haven't... well... I mean... how do I put this?... you haven't seen the *best parts* of ugliness." He giggled softly. Blushed. "I mean... well, that is... if you open your eyes to the *best parts of ugliness*, then there are answers. Better answers, at least, than what Mr. Suicide can offer."

"What the fuck are you talking about?"

He handed you the manilla envelope. "Mr. Suicide isn't my Master." He giggled. "There's something better out there. Something... I can't quite find the right words... but... well, something *heavier*." He shook his head, correcting himself. "No, not something, some*one*. Some*one* heavier." He chuckled. "Some*one* grander. The *grandest* Someone of all. And the road to meeting Him starts with taking a look inside this envelope. He told me to pass this on to you, and I must always obey Him. You know. What I mean is, obeying... that's the only choice. You know?"

Then he giggled some more. Blushed. Looked inside the envelope. Scratched his neck. "I looked inside the envelope and liked what I saw there. Liked it so much, I kind of over-used it. Apologies for that, in advance."

"Again, *what the fuck are you talking about?*"

"J-just look inside the envelope, okay? But promise me something: you have to hide it. Don't let Mom find it or else we'll both be in big trouble, okay? Do I have your promise?"

"Don't let Mom find what?"

He shook his head. Cleared his throat. "The e-envelope, dumbass. Hide it someplace she won't find it. Maybe in your closet? I dunno. I mean, after all the stunts you've pulled, she might try to search your closet to prove you aren't taking drugs. I think they're worried, you know, about you taking drugs. Anyway, all I mean is… put it someplace she won't find it or both of us are gonna be in a lot of trouble, okay? I hid it in my baseball card album on my book shelf. Tucked it into the inside pocket, and no one has found it yet, you know?"

You didn't have a baseball card album anymore. You'd thrown yours out years ago. But you nodded and told him you'd find a place for it.

"Okay," he said. He smiled. Looked relieved. "And, like I said, apologies in advance for over-using it. I mean, I don't mean to be gross or anything. Please don't think I'm gross. It's just… I wanted to share this with you because it offers another way out. The new Someone I've been talking to, He coordinates it all. Just imagine: there's a way out besides Mr. Suicide. Isn't that swell?"

He'd said the word "swell" unironically.

You put your hand in the envelope and felt glossy, slick paper in there. A magazine.

Your brother blushed deep, deep red. "Not with me in the room!" he blurted out. He'd unintentionally raised the volume of his voice so high you had to shush him. You heard footsteps approaching from the kitchen, the knickknacks rattling with each step.

Your brother rushed out the door, slamming it behind him. "I'm sorry. Oh, my, I'm so sorry. She heard me, I'm outta here."

"What's all the commotion!" Mom snarled. "My two little boys are goofing off, eh? I suppose that means you have too much free time." She knocked on your door. Five quick, hard wraps of her fist against the cheap wood. She called your name.

"Yeah," you replied.

"How many days has it been since you scrubbed the bath-tub?"

"I did it yesterday. It won't need scrubbing again until the weekend."

"If you have time to horseplay with your brother, then you have time to scrub the tub."

"We weren't horseplaying," you yelled through the door.

"Then what were you doing? Talking about me? That was it, wasn't it? You and your brother getting together to commiser-ate about how awful it is to live here, huh? Is that it? Telling each other how bad your childhoods have been?"

(Where did she get *that* idea? That was a paranoid leap, even for her.)

"Well, let me tell you, Mr. Faggot-child, you don't even know what a bad childhood *is*. Let me tell you, sometime, a few sto-ries about my old man. I wish I could tell 'em, too, but you know what they say—never speak ill of the dead. You know, that's the good thing about being dead, I suppose, no one can run you into the mud anymore, on account of it's considered impolite. Anyway, where was I... oh yeah, the bathtub! I want to see it sparkle. Make it sparkle as much as you do, you little faggot. Now!"

So the honeymoon with your mother was over. Just like that. You counted your blessings that it had lasted as long as it had. It was the longest cease-fire the two of you had ever enjoyed. "Okay, okay, I'll do it."

The oven beeped. And beeped. And beeped.

"Oh, my Lord," she hollered with inappropriate panic. "My casserole... "

Saved by the bell. She would be distracted long enough for you to at least get a glimpse of the glossy pages inside the en-velope. You rushed, fished it out.

It was a low-budget pornographic magazine called *Perfect Monsters*. The geriatric, female amputee on the cover was naked, heavily wrinkled, emaciated and attempting to insert her detached artificial leg into her butthole. You felt your face begin to burn with embarrassment. Oh dear, your brother *was* truly mad. This magazine was the thing that saved him from suicide. To him, *this* was "salvation".

You hid the magazine in between your mattress and box spring and went to clean the bathtub. You had to make it sparkle.

VII

The tub didn't need more than ten minutes of attention, but you gave it fifteen so Mom wouldn't think you were slacking off. When you leaned down to scrub nonexistent stains, the scent of Ajax stung your nose. Burned your throat, even. It was a distracting smell that got your mind off of things. It smelled fresh and clean but also toxic.

Then you were called to dinner. Tater tots and green bean casserole. There was a humid, sour smell permeating the kitchen in the wake of the casserole being taken out of the oven. The Ajax had looked and smelled more appetizing. The tater tots oozed grease. One or two of them on the edge of the cookie sheet had started to burn, lending them the appearance of dog shit.

This time, you managed to eat a little quicker than your brother did. You almost gagged, but you didn't. On your way out of the kitchen, you offered to help with dishes. Mom declined. In between bites of casserole, your brother flashed you a knowing grin. It made you uncomfortable. You walked to your room.

After a few minutes, you heard your brother finish his dinner and stride down the hallway to *his* room. Then you heard the

70

kitchen sink running. But you didn't hear any clanking dishes after that. Instead, Mom waddled out to the living room and clicked on the television. Through the walls, you could hear her listening to the news.

You pulled *Perfect Monsters* out of its hiding place, plopped onto the bed, flipped it open, and took a look.

You had, of course, seen pornography before. You had some inkling of what to expect. The women would be young and blonde, with doe eyes and full lips. They'd have nice, big tits. They'd be fingering themselves or kissing each other.

But the pornography in *Perfect Monsters* featured amputees, primarily (with a handful of other ghastly deformities thrown in the mix alongside one or two burn victims, as well). As you flipped through the pages, you felt revolted at the sights (and felt justified in that revulsion). Not only were the subjects un-appealing, but the acts in which they were participating often made you wince. A set of female conjoined twins strangled one another, apparently fighting for the right to suck a single, thin, wrinkly, old cock attached to a pelvis mercifully kept off camera. A "pinhead" (like the ones in that old movie, *Freaks*) used the crown of her noggin to stimulate a morbidly obese woman's butthole.

You gulped. Felt your heart start to hammer heavy in your chest. Your cheeks burned with embarrassment and shame. You felt like you shouldn't flip any more pages. You felt like you should throw the magazine in the trash or, better still, burn it. That was, after all, what any sane person would do.

But you didn't. Instead of doing what any sane person would do, you flipped more pages and... well... *and then there were the hanging people.* A half dozen of them, all suspended on meat hooks spaced mere inches apart from one another, like cattle. They boasted various degrees of undress and deformity.

As they bled to death, they wrapped their legs around one another. The photo captured them mid-grind. At least two of the women seemed too pale to still be alive. At least two of the men appeared to have ejaculated.

Speaking of men, that was another of the differences between *Perfect Monsters* and porno-as-usual. There were a lot of dudes in there. You flipped past those pictures. You told yourself you didn't swing that way. You began to wonder if your brother might at least partially swing that way, because the pages that prominently featured men seemed to have endured the most wear. (*Two gay burn victims, biting newly-sewn skin grafts off of one another. A mustached man blissfully sucking the exposed ligament in a recently-severed hairy foot.*)

Stains smudged the photos on those pages. You told yourself they were baby oil stains. Then you flipped another page.

This one had plastic toys of various sizes engaged in coitus with one another. Military action figures (all male) humped superhero and superheroine alike. Anthropomorphic cars and planes banged legless Barbies. Puppets extended their wooden limbs to lecherously grope Lego men. Robots tore each other to pieces and then a rubber chicken humped the pieces. You were caught off-guard by the caption at the top of the page. In fact, it broke the tension. Made you laugh. It was just a single word.

BETTER?

Yes, compared to the hideousness you'd just surveyed, the action figures were—indeed—better. Funny little mag, this one. You turned to the next page, and discovered nothing but a white page with big, black lettering.

BRACE YOURSELVES! OUR CENTERFOLD (ON THE NEXT PAGE) IS *BETTER STILL*

THE HOTTEST OF THE HOT

THE *ONLY* IMAGE IN THIS MONTH'S *PERFECT MONSTERS* WORTH JERKING OFF TO

(IF YOU SHOT YOUR LOAD EARLIER YOU'RE JUST A SICKY-SICK, NOW AREN'T YOU?)

ALL *FASCINATING* PEOPLE AGREE; THIS CENTERFOLD'S THE BOMB!

You felt yourself gulp, involuntarily.

So all of this was a joke? That had to be the case. A sick joke, surely. (Or, as the editors of *Perfect Monsters* would likely have called it, a "sicky-sick" joke.) But, yes, undoubtedly, you would turn the page and there would be a standard-issue, hourglass figure awaiting you with come-hither eyes. She'd be sitting there, totally nude, legs spread so you could see everything. And then you'd giggle and say to yourself that it was worth wading through all the disgust, to see such a hottie.

But when you turned to the next page, you were disappointed. There was some… mistake. The page was black. It contained no photo. It didn't even have any print on it. Then you realized that center*fold* meant it was a poster that was long and had to be un*folded* from the rest of the magazine. You let out a sigh of relief and proceeded to display the centerfold in all her glory. But instead of the curvy blonde, all you saw was more blackness. Three pages worth, this time.

Another joke (and this one, not the least bit funny). You felt cheated. You searched the floor; you searched in between your mattress and box spring, thinking that the actual centerfold must have fallen out of the magazine. That had to be the case. This couldn't be the actual centerfold.

You wondered *where* your brother stumbled onto this peculiar rag. And *what*, exactly, had he found in those pages that offered anything akin to salvation.

The magazine explained nothing. "Mr. Suicide isn't my Master," he'd said. "There's something better out there… No, not something, some*one*. Some*one* heavier. Some*one* grander. The *grandest* Someone of all. And the road to meeting Him starts with taking a look inside this envelope."

He was crazy, and that was all there was to it. You'd known that before, but you'd listened to him, anyway. Listened to him because he'd heard Mr. Suicide, the same way you had, and because he seemed to know of something better. But what was better about this? When *Perfect Monsters* wasn't being grotesque it was being enigmatic. You told yourself that neither quality appealed to you. You wanted to return this magazine to your brother and have nothing else to do with it.

But then you felt your brain fog over. You were suddenly drained of energy. Wanted to sleep. *How odd*, you thought. It was early, still, wasn't it? You looked at the red numbers on your alarm clock. They told you it was already 10:30 pm. You'd been absorbed in the magazine for over four hours. You should've gone off to brush your teeth, but you didn't have the power to get up. You made a half-hearted effort to hide *Perfect Monsters* under your mattress again, but your arms and legs wouldn't cooperate. You flung off your glasses then surrendered to the paralysis of something you reckoned to be sleep.

***

Then came the dreams. At least, you're pretty sure they were dreams. But they were more real than any dreams you'd ever had. For that matter, they struck you as more real than the vast majority of waking days you'd endured.

In the first dream, Siamese twins were fighting for the right to suck you off. Each one took her gnarled, muscled hand and wrapped it tight around the throat of the other. You cheered them on. "C'mon, bitches, fight for it. Fight for the right to suck off your man!"

They did as you commanded, intensifying their struggle. You got even harder, watching them strangle themselves. They winced with pain and whimpered with unsatisfied desire. Then, simultaneously, they twitched. A foul smell hit the air. Like exhausted wind-up toys, they slowed to a halt. Their eyes became dull and stationary, like those of dolls.

You giggled. "Well, damn... you both fought a good fight, only to come up empty. We can't have that. So how about this... you're both winners." You then proceeded to fuck their common twat.

The rest of the dream (if, in fact, it *was* a dream) consisted of the rest of the vignettes from *Perfect Monsters* fleshed out, similarly, in three dimensions—with textures and tastes and odors and sounds. *You* were the one anally stimulated by the pinhead (oh, how she giggled; oh, how she muttered lunatic nonsense). *You* were among the rutting meat hook people (oh, how *like a game* it was; the other bodies were so slick with sweat and blood; to grab onto them took no small amount of skill; and you did *so* need to grab on to them so you could fuck as you died). *You* were one of the burn victims biting grafts off one another (oh, the taste of it; not like chicken skin, at all... more rubbery; more bitter). *You* were sucking the ligament of a severed, hairy foot (oh, how it fit inside your mouth like a thick Asian noodle).

Your dream-self delighted in these experiences—he frolicked and laughed and groaned and came. But part of you—the part of you that suspected *you were* dreaming—felt sick at it all; resisted. You wanted no part of these scenarios. You were *not* a pervert. You were *not* attracted to freaks. *Wake up*, your aware-self demanded. *This is not me that I'm watching. I'm not like*

this. I'm not like this at all. Your aware-self tried to seize control
of your muscles; tried to flail about to force yourself awake.

Instead, the scenes repeated. Siamese twins. Pinhead. The
meat hook people. Burn victims. Foot ligament.

Make it stop. This is crazy. Make it stop. I'm going crazy.

But the scenes didn't stop, they merely changed. And not
for the better. The foot ligament morphed into a marionette
string. You found yourself suddenly imprisoned within a box,
unable to move anything but your torso, arms, and head. You
were a jack in the box. A jack in the box engaged in cunnilin-
gus with a marionette.

A robot voice egged you on. "Yeah, jester… that's how we
like it. Please her, jester. Please her good."

Make it stop. Jesus Fucking Christ, make it stop.

And then there was nothing but blackness. You *were* blackness, and you *breathed* blackness. You were just a mote of
blackness drifting through a black sky. You'd had a hard-on
this entire dream, but now it grew *exceedingly* rigid. You felt
yourself compelled to rut against the darkness surrounding
you. And you did. And it was so tight and so warm and you
bucked your hips into it. Grinding.

"Take me…" you mumbled. "Take me, *please?*"

You were begging. Whimpering.

And this time, the part of you that suspected you were dreaming didn't want it to stop. So you didn't. And thus, things progressed to the point of climax. And you let out soft moans.
And you twitched and accelerated the rate of your thrusting.

And you woke to find you'd had a wet dream, prompted
by the most wretched of porno rags. Part of you now understood why your brother had considered this salvation. Another
part of you felt disgust at what you were becoming. *This is
too much*, you thought. *This is batshit loony toons. I'm going to*

throw this in the trash, at school. Wait until no one's in the lunch room then fling it into one of the huge trash cans. I'll take scissors to it, first, so no one can even tell what the pictures used to look like. I'll cut it into tiny, confetti-sized pieces.

You told yourself you were going to do all of those things. And you felt good, felt almost-sane, almost-human again after having told yourself you were going to do all of those things.

Yes, that's just *what I'll do. Destroy* Perfect Monsters *today.*

But you didn't.

VIII

B y the time you were seventeen and in your senior year, you'd long considered yourself the occupant of the very lowest rung of the social hierarchy at school. But that wasn't true. It wasn't that you stood on the lowest rung of the ladder. No, you weren't even *on* the ladder. You were the one in the shadows, looking at the ladder. Looking at the ladder, and wanting to kick it over.

Once, you considered having a chat with the school guidance counselor. Despite the advice of the Marine at the assembly, you weren't going to tell her everything. You didn't want to get sent to the funny farm. You just needed to let the hurt out a little. And since "counselor" was part of her title, you thought she might at least listen to some of what you had to say (if only because she was *paid* to listen).

You were on the verge of scheduling the appointment. Then you remembered all the reasons you'd hesitated to confide in her. Louisville was nothing more than a big small town. She went to the same church your family had gone to in years past. You'd stopped going years ago, but your mother still went about twice a month. If you told the guidance counselor even a little of the story, she might drop hints to the pastor that you were in need of healing. And if she dropped hints to the pastor, he might tell your mother. And if he told your mother, you'd never hear the end of it. She'd scream at you for airing the family's dirty laundry. She'd accuse you of telling lies.

So instead of telling the guidance counselor what was really going on, you stifled it. The anger and pain had no place to go. It rotted inside of you. It rotted inside of you until you fucked a girl for the first time.

Yeah, that's right, fucked a girl. You fucked, to be precise, the girl who *was* on the bottom rung of the school hierarchy. Her name was Cressida and she was the girl who wore crutches (the one who put her head down on the lunch table when you were thirteen and the jock was punching you).

She hadn't gone to elementary school with you. She'd only joined you in seventh grade, so no one knew all of her back story. She'd only divulged one fact about herself: that she grew up in New York. But that was no shocking revelation. Her accent gave her away.

She wasn't from Louisville. She was an intruder to the tribe. This alone would have made her a *likely* target for ridicule and gossip at the bus stop. Her disability *insured* it.

She lived in your subdivision but didn't take the bus. Her mom drove her to school each day, on account of she had a van with a special lift to help her get in and out. Her mom drove her home each afternoon (dropping her off, getting her settled, and then driving off in the van to her waitressing gig).

It was a piece of shit van, always backfiring, but some charity had souped it up with the lift. There was a magnetic sign on the back of the van that advertised the fact that the charity had donated it. You wondered if that was a string attached to getting it, like a corporate sponsorship sticker on a race car. You figured it had to be humiliating for her parents to have to advertise they couldn't afford the lift themselves. In your neighborhood, that was like wearing a giant "kick me" sign.

So kids gossiped about how poor her family was (ignoring the fact that you were all, by any objective standard, white trash). They gossiped about how ugly she was. The boys at the bus stop teased each other by accusing each other of having a crush on her.

"I'd fuck a squirrel before I'd fuck her," one of them had said. And, somehow, Fuckasquirrel became her new nickname.

Once the kids at the bus stop tired of commenting on her appearance, they moved on to trying to determine just how she'd become handicapped.

Some kids said her legs had been mangled after a crazy car wreck. Other kids said she got that way after surviving a fall out of a window. Yet another theory was that she'd been shot (by her father, by her brother, by a burglar, by a kid at her other school, the permutations were endless).

You didn't know how she got that way. You didn't care how she got that way. All you knew was that she hobbled around when she walked. All you knew was that she only managed to get around your school with the assistance of heavy, clanging metal leg braces and heavy, metal crutches.

She could've been a model for *Perfect Monsters*.

You had, before then, always silently agreed with the other boys that she was unattractive. But in the autumn of your senior year, your assessment of her began to radically differ from theirs. You never said it out loud, of course, but her disability began to consistently give you a boner. There was something about her handicap that aroused you.

This wasn't just something in a magazine anymore. You had the fetish in real life. You liked the idea that she was hobbled. It was like Mother Nature, herself, had placed shackles around her legs. That bondage... that vulnerability. That sense of being easy to master. That sense that she needed someone to take control of her.

It took a long time for her to navigate the school, with those crutches. None of the other kids wanted to slow down to her speed to go from one class to another, so she was always walking around alone—a good ten feet behind the other kids in her class as they traveled from one room to another. This isolated her, and you used it to your advantage.

One day you pulled alongside her, kept pace with her, and asked her—straight up—if she hated the fucking cool kids. She looked over at you like she resented the intrusion into her unhappy but stable arrangement of solitude. She let out a short, sharp laugh that was intended to serve as sufficient response, and then she tried—in vain—to accelerate her pace. She walked away from you. She was wearing a skirt and you found the sight of her misshapen, atrophied leg muscles delicious as they struggled to go faster.

You, of course, had no problem matching her pace once again. You leaned over close and whispered into her ear. Told her *you* hated the fucking cool kids, and that—if she wanted—you'd fuck 'em up real good, for her sake. "All you have to do," you whispered, "is give me a sign, and I'll do it. I'll fuck up whichever one you want me to fuck up, because I don't have anything to lose anymore, you know?" When you whispered in her ear, you got a whiff of her hair. It smelled like medicinal cream.

She replied to you. Not in a whisper, but in the soft, quiet tone of voice timid people often use. "For real?"

And you assured her that, yes, you would, because the two of you had something in common. Neither of you *belonged*. One thing led to another. She said she didn't want you to beat anyone up, because she didn't want you to get into trouble over her. But she said she appreciated the offer. This led to more conversations during school. Which led to more conversations *after* school. Which led to… an emotional state that was the closest you've ever come to what most people would call "love". It wasn't love, of course. Even *you* know that. More like lust, seasoned with an obsession for ownership. You wanted to possess her—body and soul. That aura of sickness surrounding her… you *felt* it. You wanted *to be one* with it.

There was a brokenness about her that resonated with the brokenness inside you. You suspected you were diseased in your mind and possibly in the very core of your soul. Fucking her was like fucking disease, itself.

Despite the fact that she was lame, you were—in a metaphorical sense—able to get her to hop off the bottom rung and join you in the empty, engulfing darkness that lingered just away from the ladder. At least, for a month or two (September and the first couple weeks of October). You fucked her seven or eight times during that stretch, over at her house. Both of her parents worked in the evening. Your mother voiced no concerns about you going over there, probably because you'd told her Cressida was disabled (and she, like everyone else, falsely assumed she was asexual). You told her you were staying over there to study.

Fucking Cressida made things a little better. When you pounded your hips against hers and dug your nails into the tender flesh of her shoulders, you felt alive again. But then she stopped fucking you. One night she called and said she didn't want you to come over any more. She was sniffling, like she'd been crying. Said you shouldn't even *call* her ever again. Said last time you'd come over, you'd hurt her. Her mom had noticed the bruises and scars when she helped her get out of the bathtub, then asked what happened. She went crazy when she found out. Screamed at Cressida. Slapped her. Threatened to slap you, too. Threatened to have a good long talk with your parents.

But you didn't get in trouble. You never worried, at all, about getting in trouble. You figured Cressida's parents would be too embarrassed to raise the issue with your parents, and you were right. They were embarrassed of having her as a daughter. You suppose that if they could have killed her and gotten away with it, they would have. But, from what you've heard, no one can kill a kid and get away with it. The cops take that shit seriously. Cressida's parents must've known that. That must've been why they just slapped her around, and didn't go ahead and kill her. That must've been why they did the best they could to forget about it all.

Moreover, they couldn't really do anything about you having fucked her. You never *raped* Cressida. Every time she'd gotten it from you, she'd wanted it. She liked not being a virgin anymore. She liked getting a boy's attention. But she couldn't keep up with you, when it came to sheer ferocity. She sort of… gave out. She had no stamina. She got squicked when she felt a few drops of blood trickle away from her shoulder and down her arm. You were disappointed. She wasn't like the girls in *Perfect Monsters*, who were willing to go to any lengths for experience. No, sadly, she wasn't like that at all.

Damn, you wanted to kill her when she broke things off. But you didn't. You hit things—the wall, the desk, the bureau. You hit things and pretended they were her. But you didn't kill her. You told yourself she was just a receptacle, nothing else. Replaceable. You would move on to other conquests. Get her out of your head.

Somehow, though, word got out that you'd fucked her and the whole thing became fodder for drama. This made it impossible to get her out of your head.

You wondered how everyone had found out. Pieced together a likely way it unfolded, step by step. Maybe the neighborhood kids had seen you walk over there and leave. Maybe they'd noticed the way your hair was dripping with sweat or the way your shirt tail hung out of your pants afterward. Maybe they'd broken convention and slummed down to the lowest rung of the ladder and asked her what was up. Maybe Cressida had felt flattered by the sudden attention from those even slightly more popular than herself. Maybe she'd told the story in lurid detail. Maybe she'd shown them the scars (exaggerating things a little when discussing them, to keep everyone listening).

In any case, when she started yapping, everyone in the school—kids, teachers, hell, even *janitors*—cringed when you walked by.

Sometimes, you almost *liked* that. Before the news leaked out, you'd not even been in the same world as all the other kids. Now, there was finally some fact about you that made you relevant again: an action you'd taken against someone on the lowest rung of the ladder that somehow served to remind *everyone* on the ladder that you existed. Fucking Cressida made you notorious.

You noticed that girls, in particular, glared at you with revulsion and awe. On the colder days when you actually bothered going to the lunch room (instead of eating out in the courtyard), you noticed Cressida suddenly had a group of friends to hang out with. Marching band girls, mostly. The sort of not-too-dumb, not-too-bright kids who hung out with her because they felt *someone* should hang out with her to make sure she didn't fuck you—or anyone *like* you—ever again.

Seeing her like that, surrounded by self-proclaimed protectors, pissed you off. You wanted to say hello. But the one time you summoned up the courage to approach her, the gauntlet of marching band girls gave you the hairy eyeball. The leader of this clique—a redhead—spoke up and actually told you that you needed to leave Cressida alone.

Was that really what *Cressida* wanted? You didn't think so. She didn't speak up that day, one way or the other. But you didn't press the issue. You blew her a kiss. Thought that might cheer her up. Then you walked off to an empty table that was relatively close by so you could keep an eye on her.

She looked so mopey. You suspected she was just as depressed about the breakup as you were, because she'd gained weight and had taken to wearing even frumpier outfits than she had before. Oversized tops. Knee-length sweater jackets. Skirts that went all the way down to her ankles.

Winter was cruel. It gave girls the right to walk around without showing any skin. And Cressida had started to use the season as an excuse to start showing less flesh than a nun would. It was like she was doing everything she could to make herself as uninteresting to boys as possible.

To compensate for her appalling lack of cooperation with your ogling, you treated yourself to an evening masturbating in your room to *Perfect Monsters*. Eventually, you put the magazine aside and relied on your own, fresh fantasies to masturbate to: mental images of beating Cressida. Beating her *with her own crutches*. *Fucking her* with her own crutches. Sometimes, in the fantasies, other girls' faces appeared on her body. The same crippled legs, only attached to a stunning face—full lips, a slight nose. Cat eyes. You imagined band girls' faces on her body, and jacked off. You put cheerleaders' faces on her body and jacked off.

Hot stuff, but there were only so many times you could wank before it exhausted you. The skin on your cock started to chafe. You'd run out of Vaseline, and didn't want to go to the bathroom to grab another handful. You felt too exhausted to get up and shower. More and more, you drifted into a life free of the convention of hygiene.

You lay there as the cum dried on top of you and looked at the wall and heard the humming of house sounds—electricity coursing through filaments, ceiling fans slicing through the air. For years, Mom had been threatened by the thought of you growing up. She worked to keep you there in that house; in that artificial environment where sweat and grime were washed down showers and shit was flushed down toilets and cum was washed off with a wash cloth, which was subsequently laundered, then re-used to wash off your mother's face. The house was a place built on the premise that sweat and grime and shit and cum were altogether undesirable and needed to be eradicated.

And yet there was something about the smell of body odor that you *enjoyed*. That tangy scent that came with two-day-old sweat was, to you, a pleasant one. It made a statement. It said you didn't care about what other people thought. And cum… hell, cum was the stuff we'd all started out as, right? If anyone felt disgust at the thought of cum, it may have been because—in their subconscious—they felt disgust at *themselves*. Now *shit*, admittedly, you weren't so crazy about. And yet… what dude hasn't wanted to poke his cock into a chick's tight asshole? (If for no other reason than just to see what it's like?)

The house was an unnatural environment. Artificial—as in, living there day in and day out was a true *artifice*. Living there day in and day out was, increasingly, a denial of your burgeoning identity. You *weren't* conventional or kind or clean or civilized or intended to live in such a setting. Conventions and kindness and cleanliness and civilization were lies—public performances intended to convince everyone that they're not just biological entities that secrete and excrete and squish and gush. Public performances intended to fool every man into avoiding the fact that his most excruciating preoccupation is that of finding an attractive container to gush into. In your case, the most perfectly hobbled, *misshapen* container for your cum.

So, you didn't shower. You stopped brushing your hair. You stopped brushing your teeth, welcoming the corrugated layers of plaque that began to grow there. Night after night, you let the cum dry atop your skin and your jeans and your shirt.

"What do you want to do after you graduate?" you imagined the guidance counselor asking.

"Go mad," you imagined replying.

You imagined that conversation, and it made you laugh. Then you daydreamed a little more. Imagined what it would be like to sneak into her house one night when her husband was away on a business trip. Sneak into there and break her legs and jack off while she howled in pain and twitched on the ground. Then you'd come on her face, in her cunt, up her ass. Then you'd laugh and ask her, "What do you want to do after I'm done raping you?"

It's not that you hated the guidance counselor. It's more that you hated everything she stood for. She wasn't the personification of the ladder, but she was definitely a *travel agent* for the ladder. She was fully invested in the idea of advancing one rung after the other, of that procession having an intrinsic meaning. You only fantasized about raping her because you fantasized about the day when people heavily invested in the ladder finally realized its meaninglessness. You wanted people on the ladder to see that the ladder couldn't protect them from running afoul of rapists, that the sense of security conferred by the ladder was a *false* sense of security. You wanted people to finally recognize that it was those who somehow existed *off* of the ladder who had value.

It makes you embarrassed to recall that you felt that way back then: that you wanted people to value you and others like you. You're embarrassed because it makes it seem like you cared about what other people thought. You're embarrassed because it was naïve.

They would never admire you. The closest you'd ever come to being admired was being feared. Your newfound disregard for hygiene and your reputation for deflowering Cressida only reinforced your status as an outsider. When people passed you in the hallway, they gave you a wide berth. If you'd said "boo", all the other students would have shuddered. If they could have voted on "Senior Most Likely to Wipe Us All Out with an Uzi," you would have won.

You could have lingered around like that. Could have fed off that fear for a good while. It would have been better than, say, dropping out and being stuck at home. But you weren't the kind of kid who got off on playing small time, high school boogeyman. You deserved to swim in a larger pond with far more exotic fish. A grander destiny awaited you. You yearned for salvation.

IX

You were supposed to graduate in mid-June. Really, you had no right to graduate. Even when you attended classes, you put forth little effort. But everyone wanted to see you gone, so they made all sorts of accommodations on your behalf. F's became D's. Rules were bent. The principal and teachers must have put their heads together and decided that anything and everything should be done to arrange it so they'd be rid of you.

Little did they know you'd be gone sooner than they'd expected.

Yes, you were supposed to graduate on June 13th, 2015. But you *turned eighteen* on April 22. *That's* the date you'd been watching for years, and its approach made you nervous. It was time to put up or shut up. Were you going to have the guts to leave behind your mother and the artifice she inflicted on you, or were you going to stick around until your name was called out from a stage on a football field, and you picked up a piece of paper that verified you were—in fact—part of the ladder?

On the night of April 21 you were so tense you wanted to vomit. Mom told you she was going to make a cake with candles on it and asked if there were any friends you wanted to invite over. She was treating you like you were fucking ten years old. You asked her if the party was going to be at a fucking fast food place, with balloons and clowns and pony rides in the parking lot. She didn't like that. Told you that you ought to mind your manners and show a little gratitude. You told her to, seriously, not bother making a cake or planning a party.

"No matter how old you get," she said, "and no matter how much you break my heart, you'll always be my baby." She looked down at the cake like *it* was her baby. She was fussing with it like it was a baby. Putting the icing on all gentle and shit. You wanted to tell her to go fuck herself with that knife and use the frosting as lube. If you'd said that, she would have slapped the shit out of you. But she wouldn't have stopped making the fucking cake. So you didn't say it. It wasn't worth the effort to say it.

So, instead of saying anything, you went to your room and lay on your bed and considered having a little fun with *Perfect Monsters*. But you were too worked up about things to masturbate. So you took off your glasses, turned off the lights, rested there in the blackness, and felt it wrap around you like a warm blanket. You still had on your street clothes. You never changed into pajamas or even sweat pants anymore. It seemed kind of stupid, changing into special clothes to sleep in. The only things you could see were the red numbers on your digital alarm clock, glowing like embers of a fire: 10:10 pm.

There *were* moments of comforting quiet when you lay there in the blackness, but they were interrupted by Mom's racket in the kitchen—cabinets opening and closing, her muttering to herself about needing to buy new candles. Then you heard the refrigerator door close and heard her march down the hallway and into her room. Heard the door close. Heard dresser drawers open and shut, as she changed out of her clothes. Then the mattress squeaked as she fell into bed.

Dad stayed up for another hour or two, watching the Cincinnati Reds lose to Pittsburgh in extra innings. Then you heard him open the refrigerator's freezer and get ice cream. You heard his spoon clang against the bowl. Heard the bowl clang against the sink. Then he, too, proceeded down the hallway to rest in bed next to your mother. You dug your fingernails into your palms and yearned for the house to finally quiet to a state of perfect stillness—no more sights, no more sounds.

But it didn't. Your father snored intermittently. The red numbers of your digital alarm clock kept advancing. *12:53... 12:54.* Each moment that progressed toward morning inched you closer to sunrise and the deadline for your decision. Why did things have to keep happening? Why did time have to move forward? Why couldn't you simply hibernate in this one dark moment and not emerge until you were ready?

12:55. 12:56.

You became teary-eyed. Thrashed around in your bed. Raked fingernails over your own arms, and liked the rawness of the resulting flesh. Then you did it to your face. Your neck. The stinging pain helped for awhile, distracted you from the torment of the clock moving forward over and over and over again. But you had only so much flesh to rake, and when you'd already scratched all the skin that was showing, you couldn't take it any longer. You got up and unplugged the clock. In a fraction of a moment, the offending red numbers faded into oblivion. It was like you'd killed them.

You were relieved to see the red lights go out. Felt, oddly, accomplished. Outside your window, evergreen branches rustled in a breeze and scratched against the glass. They made squeaky sounds. When you heard the branches, you heard something else, too.

Whispering. Coming from the closet.

You could not make out the words that were being said, but they were unpleasant-sounding. Spoken in a man's voice, not so different from your own but not *exactly* your own. You paced around your room and tried raking your nails over your arms again, but found that it hurt too much to rake skin that had already been raked. You bit your lip, put on your glasses, and turned on the lights.

The whispering didn't stop.

You walked toward the closet. Placed your hand on the door knob. Turned it. You looked down and saw your brother—the one you'd watched go insane—lying down on top of your shoes. He seemed in worse shape than the last time you'd talked to him. More disheveled. Less glued together. "It's terrible here, isn't it?" he whispered. "*So terrible* that you're going to leave, huh?"

Your breath started to huff out of you too quickly. You grabbed a hold of the chest of drawers to steady yourself. "H-how long have you been there?" you whispered back.

"Two," your brother said. Then he started sucking his thumb.

"Two hours?"

He took his thumb out of his mouth just long enough to offer up a nonsensical revision. "Seven."

"You're going to have to get out of there."

He took his thumb out of his mouth again. Strands of slobber clung to it. "It *is* terrible, of course. But if you leave *that* will be terrible, too. Have you ever thought of that? Mom without the baby of the family? Haven't you considered how... well... *extreme* her reaction might be?"

They were the most rational words you'd heard come from him that night, but they held limited sway (coming, as they did, from the floor of your closet; coming, as they did, out of a mouth that had only moments before been sucking a thumb).

"From the looks of it, you'd be able to slip into that role just fine. And, hey, how do you know I'm leaving? I haven't made up my mind."

But that was a lie. You *had* made up your mind. You'd made up your mind, *right then*, when you saw your brother sucking his thumb at the bottom of your closet. Madness ran in the family. You half-hoped to contract it, because the very word connoted freedom from all the tiresome, fraudulent priorities of the ladder. But you were *very* certain that, if you *were* going to go mad, you wanted your madness to look different than that of the infantile man you were speaking with. If you were to go mad, you wanted it to be the sort of madness that *took you away* from the house. Not the sort that tethered you to it.

Your brother shook his head. "You're lying. You're going to leave tonight. *He* told me so. And *He* would know."

"Who? Mr. Suicide?"

"Not him… the *heavier* Someone. He said He was picking you, instead of me. Said you were more deserving. More… *fascinating*. He said you were *ripe*, and I'm not. He's the more desirable of the two options. You know what I mean? I guess what I want to say is, He offers something far more complete than what Mr. Suicide offers. Mr. Suicide is like a peasant, and He's like a king. And to emigrate to His kingdom, you have to be selected, and then you have to take your passport with you. There's a whole set of rules governing it all. I would go, too, but He didn't pick me. So I can't. It sucks, but, yeah, I can't. I guess that's what I want to say. You know? You understand me? You should consider yourself lucky to be picked by Him. You should consider yourself really fucking lucky that He thinks you're so goddamned *fascinating*." And with those words, a sullen look overtook his face—a hideous, hard grimace. His whisper became brittle and hoarse. "I can be fascinating, too, you know." His eyes oozed tears onto his cheeks, and he went back to sucking his thumb.

Chosen? Fascinating? You wanted to know more, but the whole thing was too fucked up to keep looking at. You closed the closet door. You had stuff in there that would have been good to take with you when you left. A windbreaker for the rain and the cold. Extra shoes. But you decided to just let them stay in there. Your sneakers were parked by the front door. You had jeans and socks and underwear and T-shirts in the chest of drawers. Your backpack (the el cheapo one Mom had bought for you at the dollar store after you lost yours the day you played hooky) was on the floor next to your bed. You could access everything you really needed without disturbing your brother's place in the closet. You removed textbooks you'd barely opened from your backpack and replaced them with three changes of clothes and of course, your now heavily-crinkled, creased, and smudged copy of *Perfect Monsters*.

You walked out into the hallway. Strolled around the dark house. Said goodbye to it. You felt no nostalgia for the place. There was no sense of *Oh, this is the room where we spent so many Sunday pancake breakfasts* or *This is where Mom hid Easter eggs* or *That's where they put the Christmas tree each year.* There was no sense of loss, in leaving the house. Just victory. *I've won*, you thought to yourself, as you put on your shoes.

The sofa, the refrigerator, the kitchen table, the fireplace, the pictures on the wall, the knickknacks… you could barely see them in the light of the lone lamp you'd flicked on. You pushed all that stuff out of your mind. Pushed it out and embraced, instead, the darkness that obscured it.

You didn't have much money. You wondered if you should steal some from your mother's purse. It lay on the living room couch, unprotected. You looked inside. She didn't have any cash in there. You considered taking her credit cards, but they could be used to track you. You considered sneaking in to your parents' room and taking cash from your father's wallet, but you didn't want to wake him. You considered delaying your departure until you'd saved a few hundred dollars. But that was what your mother would *expect* you to do, wasn't it? That would buy her time to work against you, wouldn't it? If she saw you saving, she'd know her baby was working toward leaving and she'd find some way to sabotage you.

You couldn't permit that. So you resigned yourself to the fact that you'd have to make a go of things with less than ten bucks in your pocket. You'd fetch food out of dumpsters. Maybe get meals at soup kitchens. You'd live on the streets. It would be uncomfortable, but an improvement over your current, claustrophobic existence. Life on the streets would *be real*. There would be no artifice.

Like all dads in Louisville, your father owned a shotgun. Shooting it at an outdoor range was the closest thing to physical exercise he ever did. It was a harmless distraction; like golf or gin rummy but with self-esteem benefits neither of those games could offer. It may have been the one place he felt powerful. Bullets assailed targets *he* selected. All he had to do was pull a trigger, and things exploded in the sky.

He kept it in a cabinet, but the cabinet wasn't locked. It hadn't been locked since you were twelve. You thought about stealing it, so you'd have something with which to protect yourself. You picked it up. Stroked the barrel. It felt pleasantly cool and firm to the touch. Oddly erotic. You wanted it for your own. You figured Dad owed you something for being such a piss-poor role model. You told yourself that this could be the first installment payment in your compensation for damages.

But it was hardly concealable. If only he'd owned a pistol,

too. (But alas, his only other weapon was a bow—equally awkward.) So you put down the gun and placed it back in the cabinet.

You mulled over the pros and cons of leaving a note to explain yourself. If you didn't, then Mom would go full tilt hysterical and probably call the cops with suspicions you were kidnapped. That's how dense she was. You didn't have a lot to say to her. You grabbed a pen from a jar of pens on the kitchen table. You grabbed a small piece of paper from a pad kept near the land line, to write messages. You started scribbling.

DON'T GO LOOKING FOR ME. YOU'LL NEVER FIND ME.

And then you signed your name.

You took the note and put it on your bed. Your brother still mumbled on, his words muffled by the closed closet door. "Fascinating too… " then the smacking of lips against thumb. "Fascinating, too… "

You paced away as swiftly as you could without breaking into a jog. Down the hallway. Into the living room. Then you quickly went out the front door. The stairs wobbled beneath your feet, like they always did, and there was a moment of unsteadiness. But you did not stumble.

From front door to sidewalk, from sidewalk to street, from street to intersection, until (finally) you escaped your subdivision. You aspired to go as far away as the public transportation system could take you. There was a bus stop a few blocks away, but the TARC system didn't start running until six or seven. They had a bench at the stop, though. And so you sat there for a few hours and watched the traffic go by. At first, all the cars were night owls. You thought you recognized one of the cool kids from school drive past you. He was laughing and smoking something while grazing the yellow stripe.

Then, as time ticked on, you heard the chatter of birds and saw the first hint of light. No more party people passed you. Now they were all adults en route to work. Many were in uniforms, of one sort or another. Similarly clad people started to assemble at the bus stop. It was better, so much better, than the *school* bus stop. Nobody here called you Trash Ass. Everyone minded their own business.

When the bus showed up, the sign on top said it was the 53 Express. You'd never taken a TARC bus before. You weren't sure how it all worked. The driver was a bald, black guy. You needed to get your bearings, so you asked him a question.

"How far does this thing go?"

He rolled his eyes at you, like he was annoyed to even acknowledge your presence. You defied the convention of sullenly getting on to the bus and not making any chit-chat, and he was annoyed by the anomaly. He turned up his radio. Three loud people on some morning show laughed through static.

You took the steps up to where he sat and asked him again, louder. You'd just left eighteen years of being disrespected. You vowed to yourself you'd never be disrespected again. "How far does this thing go?"

He looked at you like you just farted. "Downtown. Market Street. Take a map if you want one."

"And all I have to do is pay a buck seventy-five?"

"Yeah. You gettin' on?"

You had no better plan.

X

The Ohio is an ugly, brown river flowing through ugly, gray towns. Sick blood coursing through a sicker heart. The Express bus traveled over I-64, granting you a view of it, and its bridges, and the southern Indiana shore on the other side. At one point, you wished for the dickhead driver to succumb to a stroke or heart attack, so that the entire vehicle—you and everyone else around you—might careen off the assigned route, past concrete barriers, and plunge into the river. That way, you could become tiny cells of sickness, at one with the sick blood.

But that desire was only there for a moment. When it passed and no accident ensued, you felt a strange sensation.

The best way you can describe it is as an *unmooring*. You felt like you imagined one of those tugboats in the river felt, after it dropped its load and left port. There was a sense, inside yourself, of drifting away. Separation. Release of burden. You had a strong intuition that you weren't simply escaping your old life (that prison cell room in Hikes Point, those clattering knickknacks on the coffee table, that insane slapping woman who gave birth to you). No... it was more than that... somehow you were escaping *life itself*, or at least, *life as you'd previously known it*. Existence would be totally different now.

This both thrilled and frightened you. Yes, home may have been a prison, but at least it had been a familiar one. Your current surroundings were decidedly unfamiliar. You were white, and Louisville was—practically—still a segregated city. Sure, the law said different. But nobody gave two fucks about the law. So you grew up mostly around other white kids with dads who worked at other factories.

As the bus moved farther and farther downtown, more blacks and Mexicans got on. You fidgeted in your seat. Scratched your head. Stared at the other passengers, then pretended to not stare when they noticed you staring. Pretended that you'd been looking past them, perhaps at some sight that loomed outside their window. You *think* that convinced them you weren't staring.

Then you leaned back and sighed. *I'm just on a merry little excursion*, you thought to yourself. *Just a pleasure-ride, that's all. A tour of a decrepit city, via public bus. What could be better?* Yes, it was like getting into a pool. It only seemed uncomfortable for the first few minutes, and then it felt good.

You looked to the front of the bus and noticed a girl in a wheelchair sitting up there. *How had she gotten on?* You supposed the bus was equipped with a special lift to take on such passengers. You must have really been worked up when you'd boarded. How had you failed to notice *her?*

Alas, probably because she was too young for you. She looked like she was about ten. The man next to her was probably her dad. Children, even the disabled ones, weren't your thing. There were laws against messing with kids and you had no interest in running afoul of them. Besides that, you simply didn't care for the looks of their bodies. Even the most deformed children retained an aura of photogenic, big-eyed baby about them. Therefore, children weren't deranged enough to hold your interest.

They had too few years of hurt under their belts.

You hoped that an older girl in a wheelchair might come aboard, but that didn't happen. So you just sat there, watching people disembark and virtually indistinguishable replacements stream on. Black, white, or Mexican, they all had the same feel about them. You didn't know any of them, but you had a sense that if you *did* get to know them, you'd like them more than any of the kids you'd gone to school with.

Not counting Cressida.

***

You took the route as far as it would go. Got out on Market Street. Strolled around for awhile, getting your bearings.

It was unseasonably warm for a late April morning. The heat seemed to melt the air itself, resulting in blurry ripples in the distance. The sun stung you. You began to sweat after only a minute.

And yet, despite the physical discomfort, there was a certain *psychological* refreshment you found in abundance. There were other people walking around, too. A good dozen of them, treading the sidewalk either alone or in pairs or in trios. You'd never met any of these people before, but just by looking at them you felt a strong kinship. These were *not* People of the Ladder. Like you, they were people who lingered in the dark a few feet away from the ladder.

Many also had backpacks. Many, also, had escaped the chains of hygiene. Some of the women looked like whores. Some of the men looked like sleepwalkers. Occasionally you saw an infant among their number and felt jealous that it would, from its earliest days, get to revel in the sort of life you'd had to wait eighteen long years to participate in.

Despite all the marching, there were no marching band girls to be found. There were no jocks, no preps, no kids who took Vo-Tech. No *ladderly* aspirations of any kind. The walking people exuded a deep, unspoken self-acceptance: this is who we are, we do not want what Ladder People want. The ladder is a lie: our world is the truth.

You followed some of them, to see where they were heading. A small group: a man and two women, all frail and white and toothless and filthy and babbling in a way suggestive of significant mental retardation. They walked for what seemed like forever, over to the public library. You didn't want their company but you were curious about what business they would transact there. The answer turned out to be, of course, none. They were getting out of the heat. They sat down at a cluster of study carrels, put their heads down, and occasionally farted and giggled. You shook your head at the waste of furniture. Yes you *were* part of their tribe, but you could make far better use of the library than they could.

The staff wouldn't let you on the computer because you didn't have a library card. They wouldn't let you have a library card because you didn't have a driver's license. So you spent the day flipping through the glossy pages of *National Geographic*. Sometimes, they showed tits. They weren't misshapen tits. They were tits on women from remote islands in the Pacific. Nothing like *Perfect Monsters*, but still interesting. You were tempted to take the issue into the men's room and jack off to it, but something made you decide not to. You supposed you didn't because you figured someone else might have the same idea, and after your run-in with Andrew-in-the-park you didn't want to see any more pervs.

So you put the magazine down. Wandered around and strolled past hundreds of books wrapped in tacky plastic dust jacket covers. Sometimes, you'd pull one off the shelf and look inside. There was a biography of a Russian composer, written sometime in the '80s. You flipped through it and saw a receipt for a liquor store, dated June of 1995. You didn't know why, but you kept it. You felt a little mischievous, like you were stealing a piece of someone else's life. If it wasn't for the fact you weren't even *born* in '95, you could have pretended it was yours.

You looked through a few other books in that row, skimming them to look for other receipts that had been used as bookmarks. Finding none, you went to the bathroom, took a piss, got a long drink from the water fountain, and went back into the heat.

You walked past a big church, a little church, an abandoned church and a bar. You walked past a soul food restaurant and a McDonald's and a Chinese place. You started to walk toward a hospital, but then turned around. You weren't sure what you were looking for, really, but you knew it wasn't a hospital.

You walked some more and started to get hungry. You paid four dollars for a hot dog and pop. It was a ripoff, but the vendor had no line at his cart and at least you didn't have to be in a restaurant with people. The hot dog looked and tasted like a turd on a bun.

Then you sauntered over another few blocks west and discovered something far more interesting: a row of strip clubs with names like The Taj Mahal, Daddy-O's, and RazzMaTazz. You walked past them and tried looking in through the window, but men guarding the entrance said you needed to show proof you were eighteen to get inside.

"That's fuckin' bullshit," you told one of them (this dude with a comb-over and a gut and five bazillion earrings). "I turned eighteen today. I just don't have a license to prove it."

"Well," comb-over dude said, "we don't want losers in here, no how. Stop botherin' me." And then he went off to basically *harass* this businessman walking past there to come in.

Then a new voice: gravelly but pleasant. "Shit, I can tell you're eighteen. C'mon over here, sir."

It was coming from a little hole-in-the-wall joint three doors down. A tall, muscled Mexican dude stood outside the entrance. An elegant black snake tattoo coiled around his thick, tight upper arm. "Hey," you said. "You talkin' to me?"

"Damn straight," the Mexican said. "C'mere."

As you approached him, you noted the name of the place: The Border Crossing. You remembered you only had a few bucks left. "How much does it cost to get in?" You started to dig into your pocket.

"Hey, hey, hey," the Mexican said. "Your money's no good here."

"For real?"

"You're kidding me, right? My boss would tan my hide if I charged someone as *fascinating* as you to come in here."

You nodded. Walked in. It was cool in there—almost cold. The scent of gasoline lingered around the place, as though it had perhaps been a former repair garage remodeled into a strip club. You smelled fresh sawdust, too. Not far from the entrance, there was a stage. An act was already in progress. A naked, elderly woman was sitting on a stool, removing her artificial leg. A tattoo of a black spider curled around her belly button. A second stool next to her was empty, except for a carton of Crisco. A pair of ancient stereo speakers were positioned on the stage (one on each side). They were playing an old jazzy rock song from the '70s. No vocals (in this part of the song, at least). Just guitars and drums and sometimes an organ, too. Not a bad tune, at all. You started bopping your head to the beat.

You took in the rest of the scenery. Fluorescent lights hung in long lines on the ceiling. Half of them were off, perhaps in some hope of fostering atmosphere. The Border Crossing had about as much floor space as your high school gym (but with a much shorter ceiling). It had been partitioned into three separate rooms by thin slabs of plywood masquerading as walls. The plywood had been crudely anchored to the floor with multiple pairs of cinder blocks. One of the rooms, on your left, off in the distance, was full of purple light. The other, on your right, off in the distance, was pitch black. That room was cordoned off with a red velvet rope and guarded by a bouncer.

The bartender (also tall, but Caucasian; bald, but bearded) smiled when you walked in. He had a tattoo of a black horse on his neck. "Hey, my man, great to see you! Welcome to The Border Crossing! Go ahead and have a seat. Ms. Francine was about to show us her little butt-fucking trick." He jerked his head in the old woman's direction. "Weren't you, bitch?"

Her head wobbled as she tried to work up an answer. "I… I… I…"

The bartender walked up the three short stairs leading to the stage. They creaked as he climbed them, and you realized at that point that the so-called stage was actually more akin to a backyard deck and had been only recently constructed. (Thus, the sawdust smell.)

Then, over the speakers, men started adding lyrics to the jazzy rock music. They sang about noise and confusion, about glimpsing something beyond this illusion. They sang about a wayward son. And about peace. And said there was no need for him to cry anymore. It was an odd choice of accompaniment for the events on the stage.

The bartender walked right up to the old woman, grabbed onto her skinny-saggy teats and twisted them. She squirmed, grunted, and lost her balance. Her plastic leg fell out of her grasp and landed with a thud against the stage. If she hadn't braced herself with the stools, she would have toppled over and broken a hip.

"You're a horny bitch, ain'tcha Francine?" the bartender said.

She looked down. You thought she was trying to glance at the floor, but instead her eyes locked onto yours. She seemed confused and afraid and powerless.

"Tell this nice, fascinating gentleman what a horny bitch you are."

She started to speak, and her voice trembled. "I... I... I'm a horned... I'm a horned..."

The bartender laughed. The wooden boards creaked once more as he walked back down the stairs. "She's a hoot and a half, ain't she?"

So damned gorgeous.

"Hey, Mr. Fascinating. Didn't you hear me? I said, 'She's a hoot and a half, ain't she?'"

And the stirring in your groin verified that she was, in fact, a hoot and a half. Two hoots, even. But you weren't quite ready to admit it to a stranger.

"Hey..." the bartender said. "You still didn't answer me. *I said*, 'She's a hoot and a half, ain't she?'"

"She's luscious," you confessed. You coughed after saying it. Choked on the words.

He slapped the table with his palm and giggled. *"Damn straight.* That's just the word for her... luscious. Ha! You a college boy or something? I mean, to come up with a word like that, so quick an' all?"

"Yes," you lied. "I'm on the Dean's List at the University of Louisville."

He nodded. "Good man. Fascinating *and* studious. Ain't

that a combination!"

"Hey," you said. "You keep calling me 'fascinating'. My brother called me that, too."

He smiled. "Well, sheesh, kid! What do you *expect* to be called? You've been Chosen."

"But for what? By who? That's the part I'm not clear about."

"Chosen to come into this place, make yourself comfortable, and check out all the stages. Not just this one, you know, but the stages in the Purple Room and the Dark Room, too. You've been chosen to visit all three, in time. I mean, there are rules about how fast you can visit 'em. Regulations, you might say. But you'll visit 'em. Ain'tcha ever heard of the Three-Fold Path?"

You shook your head.

The bartender sighed. "This is one," he said, pointing to Francine up on the stage. "The Purple Room's the *second* step along the Path. That's the one you need to visit next. And since you're a gifted and talented college kid and all, I'm sure you've already deduced that the *third* step along the Path is the Black Room. Experience all three of these places, and you can emigrate."

"Where?"

The bartender looked at you like you were joking. Giggled, then let out a huge belly laugh. Laughed so hard he started to cry. He had to brace himself against the table and take deep, stabilizing breaths. He eventually regained his composure. "Where? To a momentary communion with your Master, before He devours you. That's the whole attraction, right? That's what you want."

You started to get up. Felt a little sick to your stomach. Stammered when you spoke. "I d-don't know what you're talking about…"

The bartender stood now, too. Put his arm around you. "Hey, hey, hey chief. Calm down, it's all right. When I said 'devour', I didn't mean in any way that would *hurt*. The whole point is to *avoid* any more pain."

"So, what, in the Black Room there's a noose and a ladder? You think *that's* badass? You think that's something I haven't already considered a hundred times before?"

A strange expression overtook the bartender's face. He took his arm off you and put his hands on his hips. Gritted his teeth. "Blasphemy? Really? Right here in the Temple, out of the mouth of the Chosen?"

"You call this dump a 'Temple'?"

The bartender reared back and slapped you. His palm was meaty and calloused and heavy as it landed on top of places where just the night before you'd scratched yourself. The blow stung and burned your face. Nearly toppled you over. You swung at the bartender's ample belly in retaliation, but he grabbed your arm and twisted it behind your back.

"Mr. Suicide's the peasant. *He's* the king. Confusing the two is blasphemy. And if you don't know that, then I reckon you're not as gifted and talented as you think you are." The bartender wrenched your arm farther up your back. "Now ask for forgiveness."

"Fuck you!"

He wrenched your arm up higher.

You wailed. Began to cry. "Okay... okay... please, please forgive me." You heard those words coming out of your mouth and felt like a weakass piece of shit. "I don't know what you're talking about. This... king... I just don't know who you're talking ab—"

The bartender shoved you. You lost your footing and ended up on the cement floor.

"Here? In His temple? You're asking who He is?"

"Don't be mad... Nobody's told me. How I am supposed to know?"

"Well, then, let *me* be the first to lift the veil a little higher than it's been lifted so far, chief. He's gone by lots of names. Some call Him 'Kuk'. Others 'Erebus'. Others 'The Great Dark Mouth'. He was the formless void who existed before time and will exist after it. People have tried... oh... for *centuries* to come up with rituals to harness Him for their own purposes. Usually noble purposes, in a sense. They wanted to make *the world* go away... to make it dissolve into nothingness. But here's a secret that not everyone knows: He doesn't want to work that way. He only takes us one at a time. He talks to us: says that if *everyone* was granted the relief of non-existence, it would be unfair. Not all are deserving of such a reward and relief. He says we're all like fruit, and He'll only swallow the ones who have rendered themselves sufficiently ripe with experience. Only *they* will serve as pleasing meals.

"You see, if you walk the Three-Fold Path, the Great Dark Mouth will devour you whole—meaning He'll eat your past, your present, and your future. That's a trick Mr. Suicide can't beat. All he can do is talk you into killing yourself. The Great Dark Mouth, on the other hand, can make it so you *were never born in the first place.* Just think about that for a moment... no need to injure yourself. No pain or discomfort of any kind's involved. You won't experience any guilt, the way you would if you had to fret about the people you'd leave behind to mourn you, because there will have never been any 'you' to mourn. You won't be dying, you'll be *un-born.* You need only step into the Black Room, here at The Border Crossing, and He'll *un-birth* you."

Slowly, you picked yourself up off the ground. "So He makes

it like I never existed? Gobbles me up and leaves no trace?"

"Well, *mostly* no trace."

"Mostly?"

"As with any meal, sometimes there are a few crumbs left behind. It might be an identification card or scrap of clothing that belonged to you. It might be a lock of hair or a knuckle bone. We call these Impossible Objects—things that *shouldn't* exist, given that someone was un-born, but *do*. There's something quite thrilling about holding one of these relics. To look at a driver's license that belonged to a man who never existed, well, you can see how that would be kinda cool, don'tcha chief?"

You nodded. "Where do these Impossible Objects show up?"

"At the place of the devouring. When the Mouth devours you, there will be some little thing left over in the Black Room. Maybe a fingernail, maybe a shirt. Whatever it ends up being, we'll save it. Venerate it."

"And my parents will never see it? My brother will never see it?"

"If they did, they wouldn't recognize it, because the rest of your existence had been eaten up. I heard you say to the doorman that you don't have ID, but let's say—just for argument—you did. And let's say—just for argument, chief—that *it* was the crumb left behind after devouring. If, after you were devoured, we mailed your driver's license to your parents' house, they wouldn't recognize the photo, although the family resemblance would tantalise them. They would be baffled that the person on the license had the same last name and the same address as them. They would look at the date of birth and find it didn't resonate with them at all. They would think whoever mailed it to them was playing some sort of mean trick on them. If they thought about it long enough, they might just start to go crazy. If they took it to the BMV and tried to get more information, the BMV would confiscate it as a fake ID. They wouldn't have any record of it being issued. And that would be the end of that."

"How do you know that, for sure?"

"Because one time when the Impossible Object was a driver's license, we tried it—just to see what would happen. Surveilled the relevant players to observe their reactions. All of us here at The Border Crossing have thought about these sorts of things for a long, long time. Lots of books have been written about the Mouth. Not books like you'd see at any bookstore, mind you. Slim little things, made cheap. We circulate them among ourselves. At The Border Crossing, we sometimes perform investigations for these journals. For those of us who aren't Chosen, the closest we can come to salvation is *assisting* the Chosen and learning more of the Mouth's mysteries. That make sense, chief?"

"So by learning the mysteries, like this Three-Fold Path, the Great Dark Mouth can be made to do what you want Him to do? He can be… you know… controlled?"

The bartender raised his eyebrows. "You want me to kick your ass again?"

You shook your head.

"Then listen up and listen good: the Great Dark Mouth devours whoever He hungers for, at any given time. He's not confined by rules. If He chose to devour someone who hadn't gone through the Three-Fold Path, then He would. I repeat… He's not confined to rules. We have no control over Him. We are at His mercy. The Three-Fold Path isn't a way to *make Him do anything.* It's not a set of rules for Him, it's a set of rules *for the Chosen.* A sort of worship designed to make the Chosen ready for un-birth. It may not be the only path to being devoured.

There are rumors of other rituals—one called the Rite of Unmasking and another called the Rite of the Naked Night (just to name two). But this is the path that those of us *here* know. Does that make sense?"

You opened your head and heart to what the bartender was saying. Nodded.

Things made *so* much more sense, now. No wonder you never gave in to Mr. Suicide. It wasn't that you *wanted to live*, it's that the variety of oblivion he offered was incomplete. Substandard. Part of you knew you deserved something better. You thought about how two of your older siblings abandoned the family—abandoned *you*. You thought about the insanity of your third sibling. The way he'd sucked his thumb in your closet. You thought about your mother and your father and Mr. Chin and detention and jocks and the bus stop and Andrew-in-the-park and Cressida. You imagined all of them as nothing more than elaborate sandcastles that could be easily enough washed away by the tide of un-birth.

You thought about how—given the age difference between you and your siblings—it was likely you were a mistake. With The Border Crossing, you could undo that mistake. And you weren't the only person who would be better off. Maybe (you weren't sure, but *maybe*) Cressida would have been better off if you'd never been born, too. In any event, you felt relieved that you—out of all people—had been chosen. You weren't exactly sure what you'd done to deserve the honor. Were you really that ripe in experience? Perhaps, for your age. But you thought that if the Great Dark Mouth had wanted to feast on experience, He would have chosen an old man. Still, why look a gift horse in the mouth? The truth was, you were uniquely monstrous. There was no other student at your high school quite like you. *That* must be it: you were *one of a kind*, and *that's* what led the Great Dark Mouth to consider you ripe.

"I'd like that," you told the bartender. "I'd like that a lot."

He smiled. "Of course you'd like that. Who wouldn't? None of us asked to be born. We all suffer too much pain and humiliation in life for it to be worth living." Then he turned back to the old woman on the stage. "Ain't that right, Francine?"

"I... I'm a horny bitch," she said. While you'd been chatting with the bartender, she'd coated her artificial leg with Crisco. She then proceeded to juggle it between her two trembling hands, before dropping it on the stage. It made a loud thud. She pouted. "I'm... I'm a horned... I mean, a horny beach..."

You looked up at her again. Smiled. Picked up the artificial leg. Felt the oily Crisco cling to your fingers. Turned around to the bartender. "Hey, you mind if I help her with this?"

He took the leg away from you. "Sheesh... you're hardcore, already!" He tousled your hair avuncularly. "It's more fun to watch her try to do it herself." He began giggling again. "Especially if she falls."

You mulled it over. Nodded.

"Now, if you like *her*, you're gonna fuckin' *love* the act after her. These two Siamese twins, joined at the hip—well technically they aren't *Siamese,* they're from Nebraska, but you know what I mean—fight each other for the right to suck my old man's cock. Cori and Dori, that's their names. If you think Ms. Francine's a hoot and a half, you're gonna start *pourin' sweat* when they take the stage. Speaking of sweatin', is it just me or has it gotten kind of hot in here? You want something to drink?"

Since looking at Francine it had indeed gotten hot. So hot you had to wipe sweat off your forehead. But there were other sights you wanted to take in before bellying up to the bar. You told the bartender you'd like to walk around a little.

"Gotcha, chief. Just mind your p's and q's, you know what I mean? Don't try to go somewhere y'ain't supposed to go, just yet. I'll be here when you're ready."

You noticed, at this point, that there were no other patrons. And you realized, at this point, that you were, truly, Chosen. Francine, the bartender, the bouncer, and the Nebraskan twins Cori and Dori were there for your benefit. That thought made your erection ramrod stiff.

After hearing about the Black Room, you wanted to get close to it. As you walked away from Francine's act, the bouncer in front of the red velvet rope stopped lollygagging and assumed his post. He was a short white guy with a tattoo of a crow under his right eye. You were taller than him, and you wondered if he might be easier to whoop than the bartender had been.

You were still a good ten feet away when the bouncer yelled at you. "Chosen or not, I'll fuck you up real bad if you try to get in here before your time. There are rules, you know. Procedures. Protocol. You should go to the Purple Room, before heading here. And there's another rule—you gotta show your passport, first, to get into here."

You kept walking. Raised your hands up, palms out. "Hey, I don't want any trouble. I just want to look inside."

Then suddenly a frigid breeze blew out of the Black Room, whipping through the bouncer's hair and blowing onto your shoulder. The mere graze of the Black Room's wind made your brain grow pleasingly numb. And then you realized how stupid you'd been, to take pride in being gifted and talented. You realized thoughtlessness had its appeal. And you took joy in knowing that once you passed through the threshold of the Black Room, you'd think no more thoughts ever again.

The bouncer, however, was somehow immune to the Black Room's charms. It didn't seem to daze him like it did you.

When he saw you continue to approach he took action. He wasn't overwhelmingly strong, but he was a quick bastard. He cracked his knuckles, sprinted toward you, and before you knew it he was on top of you, getting blows in on your belly, knocking the wind out of you.

"Purple Room first," he said, through gritted teeth. "Understand? Passport first, too!" You wriggled. Tried to get him off of you. No dice. When he was done whoopin' you, you lay on the concrete floor and looked up at him and groaned.

The bartender came over and shook his head. "Damn kid, I toldja there were rules, didn't I? But you come in here, actin' all badass and shit. Maybe you're not quite ready to spend time in the Temple. Maybe you need to cool your heels out on the streets and not come back until you get your passport all situated."

The bouncer picked you up off the floor and shoved you toward a rear exit. Your heart began pounding like a racehorse in your chest. "No! Let me stay! Let me stay!"

Off in the distance, Francine declared once again that she was a horny bitch.

The wind from the Black Room still blew onto your shoulder.

You craned your head toward the Purple Room, and caught a quick glimpse of a life-size replica of a toy robot entwined in an esoterically lewd position with a life-size plastic army man.

And then, before you knew it, you were back out on the sidewalk. In the heat.

XI

You walked a good six blocks, cursing yourself for not following the rules at The Border Crossing. When you approached the downtown sports arena, a toothless, wrinkled, wide-eyed bald dude greeted you with a question: "You, too, huh?"

"What do you mean, old man?"

"They deported you. I mean, I don't want to be nosy or nothin', but I've seen my fair share of rejected immigrants, and you look like one. You look like someone who wants to be devoured. But you got turned away from The Border Crossing, didn't you?"

A businessman walked by and glanced at you. Shook his head and sneered.

You don't know why you cared about him sneering, but you did. You didn't like the fact that you cared about it. You wanted to be more like the old man in front of you. He didn't even seem to notice how the businessman had sneered. Moreover, he seemed to know much more than you did about The Border Crossing.

"Who wouldn't want to be devoured, to escape all this plastic nonsense," the old man said. He gestured toward the passing traffic, the handful of high-rise office buildings that made up the city's modest skyline. He gestured toward women in business skirts and blouses walking back to parking garages in their tennis shoes, toward men with lanyards and name badges around their necks trickling in and out of the convention center.

You nodded enthusiastically. "They said I needed a passport."

"And you don't have one, do you?"

"No."

The old man grinned. His eyes stayed wide open while he grinned. Didn't scrunch up or anything. He just kept staring at you. "You didn't even know what they were talkin' about, did you. *Did* you, you little googly-eyed stinker?"

He was an odd duck, but possibly not the oddest you'd met that day. He had a strange vocabulary, but perhaps not the strangest you'd heard that day. You felt your skin flush. You looked at the ground. Answered him. "No."

"I didn't neither, for *about twenty years*, son, I didn't. They've moved that place every week or two, for twenty years, to make it hard to find. But I've tracked 'em down the whole time. I was dogged in my pursuit of knowledge. I was dogged in my pursuit of nonexistence. Worked my ass off to find out what they meant by a 'passport'. Now, I'll tell you, freely, what it took me twenty years to find out. You see, what they're looking for is something that establishes your identity. Who you are. Where you come from. You want to see mine?"

You nodded.

He reached into the front pocket of his filthy jeans and pulled out a dental partial plate, all wiry and gummy and toothy. "This belonged to Dear Old Mom, you know. I came back home for a few days to visit her on her death bed. Grabbed it right after she passed, before my brother called the funeral home to pick her up. Boy was he pissed when no one could find it afterward. The funeral was open casket and you could tell she was missing a whole bunch of teeth, you know? Her mouth looked all sunken in. They couldn't get a replacement pair from the dentist in time for the service and the funeral home was doing all of this on the cheap. So they either couldn't make her look better or didn't bother because we still owed them a little money. But I had no regrets, you know. At least *at the time*, I didn't have no regrets. The way I figured, it would show The Border Crossing I was serious, you know." He raised the partial plate up in the air, triumphantly. His voice grew louder. More excited. "This was my mother's! It shows who I am! It shows where I come from! This should be damned good enough to serve as my passport!"

The declaration drew glares from pedestrians walking the streets to or from meaningful activities. Businessmen, utility workers, nurses—the type of people engaged in the type of work that kept the city going—scowled at the sight of half a denture being waved through the air like a flag.

He continued, undaunted. "So the day after we buried her, I walked into The Border Crossing and I showed it to the bouncer guarding the Black Room. I even visited the Purple Room first, exactly like they said. I thought I was in like Flynn. But nosiree! The bouncer looked all pissed off at me. He said, 'This passport's a forgery. It's fake, fake, fake!' Then he laughed and threatened to beat my wrinkly ass into a pulp if I didn't scurry out of there.

"But you have to understand that it's a reasonable mistake for a fellow to make. You see, when you progress far enough in the journey you get to see that *everything* looks fake and plastic and cartoony! What's the difference between a partial plate and a real tooth? None, really! But nooooooo, the bouncer wouldn't take it."

He spit on the ground, then continued. "Anyhoo it's a real

miserable existence—knowin' about the Black Room, but not being able to go there. I don't really belong in *this* world, but they won't let me cross the border. Not until I get a passport that isn't 'fake, fake, fake'." He shook his head again. Whipped out a cigarette. Took out a lighter. Sucked on the little stick. It seemed to comfort him.

Your brain tried to sort out everything you'd learned from this particularly sage derelict. His mother's partial plate had been presented to the bouncer as a passport to the Black Room, but had been rejected because it was "fake, fake, fake". So the answer—obviously—was to give the bouncer actual teeth, not facsimiles thereof. You shared this with the old man. Told him that he probably needed to give the bouncer at least one (if not more) of his mother's actual teeth. "At least," you said, "that would be a first step. I mean, that would at least answer the 'fake, fake, fake' objection. Who knows, he might be a real ass-hole and give you some other reason for rejecting the passport, but you never know, he might—"

The old man interrupted you. "For Christ's sake, don't you think I *already thought* of that?"

"Then why don't you do it?"

"Because we buried her!"

"Can't you get some other person's tooth? You know, maybe your brother's?"

He blew smoke in your face. "You don't get it, do you? Your passport provides verification of *where you come from*. And *where you come from* is your mother's belly, right? *That's* the place where the obscenity of your existence is first perpetrated! Shit, I thought they taught you kids all about how babies were made in school, right? You have to get some piece of flesh or bone, or maybe some bit of blood, that comes from *your mother*. *That's* your passport, idjit! To *take* birth from you, they need evidence—beyond all reasonable doubt—of who *gave* birth to you."

You coughed. Cleared your throat. "I know damn well where babies come from, damn near made myself one," you said. It felt good to brag about your conquest of Cressida. "Anyway, if you already know what the problem is, why don't you go and take care of it."

He stepped toward you. Glared. You noticed, for the first time, that the reason he seemed to always be staring was that he had no eyelids. This excited you. Made you tingle all over, at least until he started yelling at you. "I already told you, *my mother's dead!*"

More passers-by turned their heads toward you. But none of them were cops, so you kept on pressing the issue with him. "Why are you letting that stop you?"

"Christ, kid. What are you sayin'? That I oughta dig up my mom, unseal her vault, break open her coffin, and grab somethin' out of there? Is that what you're sayin'? Even if everything *is* fake and plastic and cartoony, some things still matter to me. I *loved* my Dear Old Mom. I mean… really, really *loved* her. I'm not gonna do that!" He looked at you like you were the biggest piece of shit he'd ever seen. Then he took three steps back, like you were the carrier of the vilest disease known to man.

Suddenly, you felt self-conscious. You didn't want the old man to walk away from you. You needed the information only he could give you. Moreover, there was the whole matter of those eyes. *Those eyes…* you felt… well—there's no other way to say it—*attracted* to them. You back-pedaled from your previously strident position. "Look, I mean, I'm just thinking things through, right? I mean, I get it—you don't want to dig your mom up. I know it sounded crazy when I said it, it's just that— well, it's just that I wanted to help you, that's all. I wanted you to be able to get a passport. I mean, you want to go into the Black Room, right?"

He coughed. "Fuckin' A, I want to go into the Black Room! I mean, look at this city. Just *look* at it. How can anyone stand it? Cars and business clothes and buildings and plastic people getting excited about a stop light that's been stuck a little too long on red, or getting excited about the games they play in this big, plastic arena. All this fuss over... *what*, exactly? Over nothing but a parade called life—a parade that starts everywhere but goes nowhere; a parade held for no apparent reason, and—worst of all—a parade that *pretends it's not even a parade*! A parade that insists that it's a natural saunter around the block. Just a wee merry stroll! Just a wee merry stroll! Oh, look at the daffodils! Look at the college basketball team! Look at your paycheck! Your car! Your body! That girl's body! Make babies! Ever more babies! Ever more plastic marchers for the parade!" He coughed some more. Hocked a loogie. "The whole thing is disgusting!"

You took in the vast parade. All the coming and going, the clip-clop of heels, the pacing, the marching, the squealing of brakes and the honking of horns, the blare of three competing strands of music strangling each other in the hot, humid air— the sickening motion of it all, the flow of bodies back and forth like waves on a river.

The sea of humanity made you seasick. You felt a deep pang of sympathy for the old man. Felt his bones as you patted him on the shoulder in a gesture of consolation. "I'm so sorry. How do you bear it?"

"I get stoned," he said, "or drunk. Whichever's available, you know. I ain't exactly the kind of guy who's picky."

You'd had lots of reasons to get drunk or stoned, but you'd never been near the stuff. Mom and Dad never kept intoxicants at the house. You suspected that most of the people in school assumed you'd done drugs, because all loners did drugs, right? How else to explain your disheveled appearance or the way your eyes never quite met anyone else's, or the fact that your grades suffered?

The irony of it all was that, *if you'd done drugs*, you wouldn't have been such a loner. You'd once researched weed, to see if it would have been a good fit for you. Had it not been for Mom's constant snooping around in your room, you would have tried it. From the testimonials you'd read on stoner forums online, marijuana could have been like a stomach medicine. It could have decreased the seasickness you felt when you had to spend time around the sea of humanity. It could have relieved the tightness in your nerves, that tightness in and around your skin, the tightness that made you feel like you hadn't been so much placed in this world as *shoehorned* into it. You may have even ventured on to the ladder, if you'd let your brain get fuzzy enough.

"Can I do some with you? Drugs, I mean."

The old man looked annoyed. "You mean right now?"

"Why not? Is it like we have anything better to do? Isn't it better than sitting around here and feeling shitty about being shut out of the Black Room?"

"You got a point, there, Junior."

"So can I?"

"How much money you have on you? I'm not running a charity, you know."

You showed him a five-dollar bill. He snatched it out of your hand. "Okay, I'll consider this a deposit." He grinned a gummy grin. "Follow me. Got a little place I use. So far, no one else has found it. Just my little nest, comfortably away from the *parade*. I have a little something there that I think you'll like."

You were not prepared for the walk that followed. Many, many blocks west. A few blocks south. The sun started to set and the shadows of tall buildings began to shift and fall around you like chopped trees. The old man slowed down as you reached a block of abandoned businesses. "My place is in the old dry cleaners," he whispered. "We should probably wait till it's darker, just to make sure. Let's take another walk around the block until then."

"To make sure of what?" you asked.

"To make sure no one sees us go inside. You see, there's no such thing as honor among bums. If they see I have a nice little nest, well, they might decide to see what's inside that I happen to find so damned comfy. They might come over and squat there, uninvited. And what am I going to do, call the police because they're tresspassin'?"

So you walked around the block. Killed time until Earth had twisted itself out of the sun's glare. And after the sun had dipped completely past the horizon the old man was still not satisfied. You walked some more. You walked until you saw the first faint star out-gleam the light pollution. You were the sweatiest you'd ever been in your life. Your feet ached. But you didn't obsess about taking a shower (that would have been ludicrous; you knew better than to expect the old man to live anywhere with running water). You didn't obsess about resting.

No, you obsessed about drinking and drugging. You obsessed about reaching a chemically induced oblivion, until you could reach the real thing.

The old man approached a door that was boarded up with plywood. "Hey," he whispered, "make yourself useful and pry this loose for me. It's not nailed on tight. I can pry the board *just loose enough* so that it stays on, but I can squeeze through. I can do it, but it takes me a long time."

You put your hand against the edge of the board and noticed it had gotten tagged with graffiti (a black squiggle of odd symbols that looked like an ancient language the world had done itself a favor in forgetting).

You weren't the most street smart kid in the world, but you were pretty sure you saw on TV once that graffiti was all about claiming territory. And surely, the old man was not the one who'd performed the tagging. So was it not likely that the old man was squatting in someone else's space? Or at least, space controlled by a gang? What if you had it all wrong? Yes, you had it all wrong! The graffiti marked the *neighborhood* as belonging to a gang, not that exact building. That was it, right? You thought you knew something about all of this, but you were *not* the most street smart kid in the world.

You took a deep breath and pulled. The board gave way, revealing a glass door with a gaping, jagged hole near the bottom. A dark mouth, ringed with glass teeth. When you crawled through, you were careless and cut yourself on the forearm. You let out a string of curses through gritted teeth. Stung like a motherfucker. The old man laughed at you. "Fucking rookie," he snarled.

You wished you'd remembered to bring first aid supplies along with you. All you could do was fumble around in the dark, take a sock out of your backpack, and tie it around the wound. You knew it would probably look ridiculous when you ventured back into the light, but you wanted to save your clean T-shirts for something besides mopping up blood.

After the old man climbed in after you, the plywood rested back in place. The inside was cool and smelled like chemicals that had once been intended to clean but had somehow even managed to go rotten, themselves.

The old man collapsed onto the floor. "I'm gonna rest for a

bit."

You knew why he was resting. Your muscles demanded rest, too. They'd been on the verge of mutiny when you'd arrived at the dry cleaning place. But you'd kept control over them and they hadn't mutinied. You didn't want to rest. You wanted to get drunk or high for the first time. You didn't want the old man to rest, either. You wanted him to tell you where the goodies were. You wanted him to teach you how to smoke the goodies or how to hold your liquor. It was like Christmas morning. You wanted to unwrap your presents. And the old man was like your dad, telling you he wasn't fuckin' *ready* to watch you unwrap your presents.

After a few minutes, he started to snore and you were alone again. You rested your back against the tile floor and used your backpack as a pillow. The floor felt dusty and hard, but you didn't miss your bed back at home. Even a drugless drug den was preferable to the artificial life you'd had to live with your parents. You listened to the occasional car roll past, its stereo booming. Pale street lamps flickered on, reaching past the loosened plywood and jagged glass, sending a splinter of light in your direction. But it didn't reach you. It fell a few feet off to your side. You were *glad* it didn't reach you. You preferred the dark.

It did reach the old man, though. It lit up the area around his eyes. The light seemed to sink inside his crow's feet, but it reflected off the eyeballs themselves. In the black room and in that pale light, against his pale skin, any trace of color seemed bold and pulsating and alive. You noted the redness inside his eyes, the pronounced veins. They seemed even worse than your own eyes, after the peroxide. You could almost see the blood *coursing* through them.

You started to get a hard-on. Those deformed, lidless, decrepit eyes—so gorgeous. You took off your pants and pulled your cock out of your underwear. Stroked your meat. That's all you wanted to do at first. Just whack off and be done with it. But those eyes... that decrepitude. He slept, surely he slept. He snored. And yet those lidless eyes had no choice but to flaunt their hideousness. You crawled over and got closer to him. What ugly sights had those ugly eyes seen in all their ugly years in this world? You jacked off more ferociously.

You were not heterosexual, nor homosexual, nor bisexual; all of these terms insisted on defining attraction in reference to one set of body parts, or another, or both. You realized, at this point, that all three orientations were useless in defining your experience. You were attracted to damage, decay, and disease and the old man's eyes were luscious with all three. You wanted to fuck brokenness, whether that brokenness belonged to a crippled girl your own age or an old bum with lidless, wrinkled, bloodshot eyes.

You scooted even closer for a better look and noticed even more redness in those eyes than you'd noticed before. Noticed how the pupil seemed unstable, as though it had gotten detached and drifted. As you masturbated with your left hand you touched his crow's feet with your right. And when your finger brushed up against the desiccated skin, you could no longer restrain yourself. You came. You shot your sperm off into the womb of the surrounding darkness. You let out an involuntary whimper.

The old man stirred. Brought his hands up to his face. Why was it that, when he woke up, you felt ashamed? You hadn't felt ashamed of fucking Cressida. You hadn't felt ashamed of masturbating while thinking about beating her. You hadn't felt ashamed of wanting to kill her. You hadn't felt ashamed of wanting to kill yourself or of having plotted—however briefly—to kill your mother. You hadn't felt ashamed of walking around unbathed and ungroomed and reeking of sweat.

What led you to feel self-conscious when the old man stirred? Was it some latent respect for your elders? The sense that the old man, unlike Cressida, represented an authority figure? Someone who knew about drugs and booze and passports when you did not? Someone who was clearly a pro in terms of navigating the streets? Was it that you knew he wouldn't understand why you'd been attracted to him? That he would mistakenly ascribe it to homosexuality, and express revulsion against you, and leave you or demand that you leave him? You weren't sure you could bear that—not now, after having just had his magnificent decrepitude revealed to you by that stray beam of pale, flickering lamplight.

Maybe you felt self-conscious because of the growing, nagging suspicion you were being watched (and *had been* watched for a long time). A sense that the darkness around you was sentient. You heard noises—a sort of mumbling that sounded like mocking. Were you self-conscious because you now felt certain the Darkness was laughing at you?

You fumbled to find the right words to explain yourself to the old man. "I, I was just looking at you," you said. "Admiring you. You don't understand. You should take it as a compliment. You're almost everything I want to be."

His hand stroked the side of his face that was turned away from you. When he brought it back up where you could see it, heavy strings of jism were draped over it. "You fuckin' perv," he gasped. He seemed astonished, and astonished *at having been astonished*. "I know Degeneracy is part of the Path but... but... in all my years out here, I've never... I'm... I'm... I'm an old man!" His voice broke and he sounded like he was going to cry. "You gotta leave now, you hear?"

You shook your head. You had no intention of going any-where.

"Look, if you don't get out of here, then I'll holler real loud. I've been out here—one place or other—for twenty-five years or so, Junior. I ain't some piece of shit flushed out onto the streets by his parents. I have friends out here who would fuck-ing cut you bad for what you just did."

"I didn't do anything to you," you said. And it was true. You had no control over the fact that your cum had fallen on him, any more than you would have had control over falling confetti.

"You fuckin' *came on my face* you fuckin' pansy!" He got up and reached into his pants pocket. Pulled out something short and stubby that glinted in the lamplight. "Shit, forget about me calling my friends. You ain't nothin' but a fuckin' light-in-the-loafers kid. I only hung out with you because I let myself feel sorry for your candy ass! I was worried that you'd be chewed up and spit out of the streets in a matter of days, without a little guidance. I can fuckin' cut you, myself. Cut out those googly eyes so they can't fuckin' faggot-stare at me all the time. How'd you like *that*?"

There had been a time when you'd have liked that very much. But that time had passed. So much had changed. You were on a path to salvation and your brother was right: if you opened your eyes to the *best parts* of ugliness, then you had answers.

You put some space between the two of you. Tried to soothe him with reassurances that none of this was necessary. You wanted him to understand that you hadn't meant any harm. You wanted to stay with him. "I think we can work this out," you said. "It's not like you think it is. Besides, you're old and I'm young and you probably need someone to help you. Like you needed me to help you with the door when we came in here. I mean, we can be a good team."

That's when you heard the old man's feet galloping over the floor toward you. "Fuck you," he screamed. "Fuck you for throwing that up in my face!" You dove out of the way—crashed against something thick and metal. Your side felt sore. The old man fell, too. Ran into the front door. Let out a yelp. Landed with a thud and a howl. *Ran into the jagged glass*, you told yourself. *Cut himself, probably on the leg.*

You got up. Noticed that something didn't seem quite right. Felt around your face and noticed the frames of your glasses had gotten bent in the collision. You adjusted them so that they sat evenly atop your nose again. Then you stood over him. The short stubby thing that had glinted in the old man's hand now glinted on the floor. You grabbed it by the wrong end and it poked you. It was a sharp knife. You were lucky you hadn't cut yourself when you picked it up. You brandished it. Lowered your voice to a soft mumble. You knew he wouldn't calm down if you weren't calm, too. "Listen…" you told him. "I mean… just listen… Shhh…"

The old man growled in between winces. You could hear him scrambling on the tile, like a bug that had been turned on its back and was unable to right itself. "Don't you fuckin' shhh me, son."

"I wanted this to be a partnership of equals," you said. "But you're fighting me too much to do that, you see. So I'm going to have to be the one who wears the pants in this relationship."

More scrambling and, for the first time, whimpers. "Look… I'll give you some of what I got… the drugs, I mean. Pills. Good stuff. Just clear out of here."

"I'll take those pills, sure, but only *with you*. Not without you. You don't seem to understand me. From now on, we're going to be together…"

"Fuckin' faggot! You clear out of here now you fuckin' fag—"

What could you do? Let him go on like that? Let him continue misunderstanding your motives? Your muscles tightened. You felt your heart knocking away in your chest. You felt flush. You felt alive. The last time you'd felt this alive you were fucking Cressida. Digging your nails into her shoulders. Bruising her. Scarring her.

What happened next was a blur (the way sex often is). Exactly what moment did the whole thing start? Who did what to whom? You remember only that there was a tumbling. There was the splinter of pale, flickering light. When he was too bashful to take his clothes off, you cut them off. You remember that. It took a very long time for him to get hard, you remembered *that*. He fought it. But your hands were soft, so his nerves responded and the old soldier cranked up, almost mechanically, little by little, to attention. And when he'd gotten good and stiff, you felt the urge to kill infuse itself into your urge to fuck. You had a sense—however delusional—that the knife was highly sensate. When it touched the old man, you felt—viscerally *felt*—pleasure: a quiver of your cock, a shiver down your spine, erupting gooseflesh. You made incisions and the old man let out primal cries in response. Howls, like those of a man who was coming. You sucked and you swallowed whatever fluids oozed forth from the wounds. Your knife and your fingers and your cock and your teeth ravished every inch of him. How could they not, with the whole banquet of decrepitude laid out for your enjoyment? You tumbled and kissed and you came in your pants and, after he'd stopped screaming and fighting, you took your pants off.

You needed little help getting hard a second time. You needed little help to come a second time. *Euphoria...* one hundred thousand needs met in the space of seconds.

You do not recall exactly *where* you came. Some hole. (A natural orifice? One of your own construction? You can't say.) You can remember being sweat-slicked and spent. You remember wiping a strand of your friend's flesh off your face, and realizing that somewhere along the line you'd lost your glasses. You remember stroking his chest hair and letting your fingertips explore every delicious wrinkle along his torso. They reminded you of labia. You wondered if they were as sensitive, for the old man, as labia were for a girl. "Coochie coochie coo," you said. You nuzzled against the web of wrinkles on his neck. Loved the feel of them against your cheek.

He didn't say anything. Your breath hitched. You put your ear up to his chest, listening for a thump. Nothing. You looked up. In the tumble of sex, you'd moved away from the ray of flickering light. You couldn't see his face anymore. You couldn't hear his heart.

A wave of tension squeezed your brain and made your stomach lurch. Sure, you'd felt the urge to kill him, but it was still a surprise when he was gone. (After all, you'd felt the urge twice before—with Mom and with Cressida—and hadn't succumbed.)

Your only friend, gone, because you hadn't had the willpower to resist the urge to kill and because *he* didn't have the stamina to withstand what it meant to be your friend. Because he *fought* being your friend. You could have had a beautiful partnership together, if only he'd cooperated. Instead, you only had this. It was what you wanted, but it *wasn't* what you wanted.

The Darkness around you chuckled.

You knew from the very first moment you heard it that it was the *Darkness* chuckling. Not *a person* in the darkness, but that living Darkness which was the Great Dark Mouth. And yet, despite this knowledge, you paid lip service to the saner proposition that another human being was in there with you. "Who's there?" you said. "Show yourself!"

The voice taunted back. "'Show yourself'? I'm showing myself all over this fucking room, bucko. If you can't see me, you're blind!" Of course, He was showing Himself. The voice was the Darkness, and Darkness was everywhere.

The chuckling only stopped when a more alarming noise cut through it. Outside, off in the distance, a police siren wailed. For a moment, you panicked. Then you giggled. Oh, how they would misconstrue all this, if they happened onto the scene. They wouldn't realize it wasn't your fault that this happened. The old man had died because he fought back when he was in no real position to fight back.

But you didn't have to worry about the police, as least not that night. The siren faded and twisted with the Doppler effect as the car careened past your hideaway.

You thought about the transition from life to death, about the threshold the old man had crossed through. It was both dramatic and subtle. When you let your hand roam, you could still feel sweat on his brow. Sweat that had trickled out when he was alive. When you let your hand drift down to his groin, you could feel it was slick and gummy with other vital fluids, once nestled inside of him, now resting atop him in various degrees of dryness. His brain and heart and lungs and the chunks of what used to be his cock no longer worked. You noticed, for the first time, the faint smell of shit. His body had expelled whatever meager nourishment he'd last taken in.

And yet, he was still a recognizable *thing*. Two arms, two legs, a head. He still had those delicious wrinkles to nuzzle against. In the darkness, you could no longer see those stunning eyes. But you knew they were still there, *still* stunning in all their beautiful ugliness.

You realized he still had value. He could still, in a way, be your friend because he wasn't gone. If he was buried or all burned up, he'd be gone. But he wasn't buried or burned up. He was changed, but—if you thought about it—only slightly. Crossing the threshold had faded him... twisted him... like the Doppler effect faded and twisted the sound of the police siren. The police siren was still a police siren, wasn't it? Just... warped, from your perspective. Changed. So your friend could still be your friend. It's just that your friendship would have to be different, now. Death wasn't a barrier for the meat hook people in *Perfect Monsters*, so it didn't have to be a barrier for you, either.

You weren't a fool. You knew that, over time, he would change more and more and that, ultimately, some of the changes might not be to your liking. But some of the changes would be wonderful. You didn't believe in God, but whispered a prayer anyway, because a prayer was the only kind of sentence that sufficed to contain your desperation. "Please," you whispered, "I know he will have to lose his flesh, but don't let any bug eat up his eyes."

The Great Dark Mouth answered your prayer with more laughter. Then He spoke. "Flesh-thing likes his flesh," He said. The voice was sarcastic, taunting, condescending. Then you could feel the Great Dark Mouth around you, as though He was a physical presence. Heavy, humid, cold. Reeking of trash and smoke. Felt Him around your neck, clenching His teeth on you like an animal displaying His dominance. You gasped for air, but couldn't get it. You began to feel your pulse throbbing away in your carotid arteries, felt your torso start to ache with the thudding of your heart. You felt vertigo. The ground was dark and the ceiling was dark and you searched in vain for that stray beam of lamplight to give you a landmark, to fix your location.

Your stomach churned. The Great Dark Mouth cackled. "*Flesh*-thing," He mocked. "Flesh-*thing*," and then you passed out.

XII

You dreamed you were in a vast desert, in the middle of a circle of towering stone obelisks. The sky had four suns—one in each of the cardinal directions—but you felt cool, because the suns were arranged in such a manner that there was shade coming from each direction. You were totally bathed in the shadows of the obelisks.

That's when you heard the voice: the one that had spoken to you before you'd fallen asleep, the voice of the Great Dark Mouth. It sounded young, like your own, but it *wasn't* your own. Not *quite*. "Listen up, bucko. *Perfect Monsters* is the *holiest* of holy books. There is only one copy of it in existence. I created it solely for you, to use as a road map and guide for *how to escape life*. It's divided into three sections, one for each step along the Three-Fold Path. Allow me to elucidate. Step One: Degeneracy. To escape life, you must first escape *society*. And the best way to escape *society* is to violate its norms in such an extreme manner that you are no longer welcome; to embrace that which humanity has been taught to turn away from and condemn: the ugly, the misshapen, the foul. After tonight, I think we can say you have performed the first step with flying colors. But now you mustn't get stuck on the first step. You know, so many people do that. Get stuck, I mean."

You scratched your head. "Stuck?"

"Yeah, you know... stuck... as in... they find the filthy, the diseased, and the decayed so addictive they can't leave it. They get addicted to fucking and they get addicted to killing. Addicted to the squishing out of cum and the gushing out of blood. They have to keep on *marinating* themselves in all that squishy-gushy! There's a fella named Dahmer I used to talk to... a promising prospect, mind you, who wouldn't move on from Step One to proceed to Step Two. You don't wanna end up like *him*, do you?"

You knew who He was talking about and no, you didn't. Dude killed and fucked and cannibalized and was a total badass motherfucker. You didn't want to end up like him, though, because at the end of the day you were a lover, not a killer. Dude landed himself in prison and some punk bludgeoned him to death. You didn't want to end up like him, because that would be too painful. "No," you said, "I don't want to end up like him."

"Good. I knew you were my kind of lad. So, you see, the trick is to—very quickly—flip the switch in your mind over to aggressively *resisting* the urges to fuck misshapen flesh and kill it. Resist them, abandon Degeneracy, and instead embrace Step Two: Derealization. You *do* know what that is, don't you flesh-thing?"

You shook your head. You didn't.

"Well, I guess that wouldn't be the sort of thing they teach in high school, would it? And, hell, even if they did, it's not like you'd remember it anyway, right? I mean, with the way you zoned out in class and all. Anyway, *derealization* is when the world around you doesn't seem so solid, anymore. When everything you thought was flesh turns out to be plastic. When everything you thought was plastic turns out to be smoke and light. When everything you thought was smoke and light is revealed to be... a mirror trick, a fraud, flimflam! It's the sense that your life isn't real anymore. The sense that it's more like a movie."

"Gotcha... Gotcha... So I have to follow the Three-Fold Path. How does all this business about a passport play into things?"

"The Three-Fold Path is a *spiritual* process. The process of obtaining your passport and taking it back to The Border Crossing is the *physical act* which facilitates it. Call it magick if you want. Call it *witchcraft*. And then the magazine, *Perfect Monsters*, let's call that a *grimoire*. Or, better yet, a *Book of Shadows*. *Now* does it make sense?"

You weren't quite sure it did, but you nodded. You felt fearful of admitting any confusion.

"Now it's your time to wake up, flesh-thing."

You didn't want to wake up. Dwelling with the Great Dark Mouth—even if just in a dream—felt too damned good. There was an ease about this place. A detachment from care. An ongoing, chill wind that blew over your brain and froze all worry. A sense of drifting away from your body like a helium balloon that was only tethered to the ground by a thin string. If you woke, you would have to deal with the consequences of... well... of what had happened earlier. If you stayed there in the shadows of the obelisks, you wouldn't.

You told the Great Dark Mouth you'd rather not wake up.

"It feels good, doesn't it? Dwelling in the shadows, I mean. It feels peaceful, doesn't it?"

You nodded.

"Well, this is only a *taste* of what you'll have in the future, flesh-thing... once the magick is completed."

"Can't you go ahead and take me now?"

The Mouth shouted. "When *I said*, 'it's time to wake up', did I sound like I was *making it fucking optional?*!"

You shuddered.

"Who do you think calls the shots, bucko? Wake up and perform the magick. Go get your passport. Proceed along the Three-Fold Path. Then, and only then, will you be ready for un-birth. So… go! *Wake!* Or do I need to make a scene to wake you?"

Then there was a rumbling in the earth, a shifting of sand, and stones rained down from the obelisks. They tumbled down with great scraping, shattering noises; and when they fell the dust whooshed into your face—up your nostrils and down your throat and against your eyes. And shards of the rocks bombarded you from all directions and you winced and you were wounded and you cried out and fell to the ground, cowering.

And yet you were still bathed in shadows. The obelisks had not fallen. Only the false *exterior* of the obelisks had fallen. Now you saw the obelisks revealed for what they truly were, at their core: towers of rotting flesh constructed with a mortar of blood and shit. They were made of body parts that wriggled against one another, sexually. A hand thrusted into a wound made in the throat of a headless neck. The neck, in turn, thrust its stump into a waiting, wet gut. The motion spilled a rope of intestines from its home, and it slithered like a snake, down, down, down the obelisk until it found a rotting mouth to penetrate.

Your cock stirred to attention at the sight. The erection offered only mild pleasure, though. Nothing compared to the sweet breeze of oblivion you'd felt blowing over your brain.

XIII

You woke with cold sweat pouring down your brow. It trickled onto the places you'd scratched yourself the night before. You wiped it off as best you could, but that just reopened the wounds. Sweat made them sting like a motherfucker. Droplets of something thicker than sweat flowed into your eyebrows. You tried wiping it away with the hem of your shirt, but as you grabbed it you realized it was too messy to be of any use. It felt sticky and still wet in some places. So you couldn't clean yourself up. It felt mighty uncomfortable.

Of course, your friend was in even worse shape. He'd gotten chilly during the night.

It was still dark in the building. The windows must have been covered by plywood. The only difference between daytime and night was that in daytime the thin ray of light leaking into the building no longer flickered. You couldn't see the condition your friend was in. You decided that was for the best. If you saw, you'd be tempted to go all squishy-gushy again. Even with the Mouth watching.

You couldn't let yourself succumb to squishy-gushy again. You didn't want to get stuck on the first step of the Path, like Dahmer had. The old man had told you a little bit about what you'd need—in the way of a passport—to enter the Black Room. The Great Dark Mouth had re-emphasized this. If you went to your mother, retrieved a bit of flesh or blood from her, and delivered it to The Border Crossing, you'd finally be unborn. But that was a paradox, now, wasn't it? The Great Dark Mouth didn't want you to murder again, but demanded your mother's flesh or blood as a passport. How could you obtain flesh or blood without any *gushing*?

You were, it seemed, in a no-win situation—but you had no choice but to move forward. You had to take some things on faith. You owed it to yourself to at least try.

What to do with your friend's body? Try, in some way, to conceal it? Where? Throw it in the trash? In time, the smell would give it away. Besides, getting all the deadweight through the plywood and glass would be a delicate trick. It would require the dead man to suddenly become a skilled contortionist. Moreover, people might see you move the body around, if you went outside. No, there was a wisdom emanating from somewhere deep in the marrow of your bones that told you to leave it where it was. Just leave it and go take your passport from Mom.

You'd need bus fare to do this, though. So you searched through the old man's pants, found found his cash, and took it.

You wanted to try to find his pills, too. You groped around in the dark for a while, but soon realized the search was futile. The old man had known what he was doing when he'd hidden his stash. Maybe there was a crumbling place in the wall where he'd hidden it, but for all your groping you couldn't find it. You felt stymied. Sure, the old man was dead, but in a way it seemed like—in the end—he'd gotten his way. You'd wanted a relationship with him, and he didn't. He'd gotten his way, there, hadn't he? You'd wanted drugs and he'd wanted to rest. He'd gotten his way, there, too, hadn't he?

No big deal, you decided. So what if he could have been able to declare a sort of moral victory out of the tussle. With some more cash in your pocket, you felt like a fucking millionaire.

A *hungry* millionaire. It had been forever since you'd eaten. Your stomach made little whining noises. "Shaddup!" you wanted to say to it. "Shaddup right now!" But it would have been pointless to yell at it. It had a legitimate complaint. It felt neglected.

Of course, there was meat right there on the floor. *Perfect Monsters* had shown you men eating skin grafts off of one another; a man sucking on another's foot ligament. Thus, cannibalism was not exactly beyond the pale for you. But that meat had been your friend and your lover and... more important-ly... you realized—after your dream—that consuming him would be squishy-gushy. It would be too much like Dahmer. The Great Dark Mouth would not approve. So you resisted the temptation to sate your hunger with human flesh. You put on your backpack, found your glasses on the floor, grabbed the old man's knife as a memento of the occasion, and aban-doned the abandoned building. Scrunched down so you could squeeze past the plywood. Cut yourself again (this time on the leg) as you wriggled out of there. You let out a little yelp.

If that wasn't enough, the sun stung your eyes when you left. It took two or three minutes for your vision to adjust. You re-alized, too late, that you hadn't been at all discreet about your exit from the love nest. The old man had been wily, had only entered under the cover of deep darkness. You rolled out in broad daylight, and made more than your fair share of noise when you did.

The moment you realized you'd slipped up, you heard giggles escape from the gap between the plywood and the broken glass door. The Mouth mocked you yet again. You yearned to be devoured by Him but you didn't like the way He treated you. That condescension. When you'd left home you promised yourself you'd never take bullshit from *anyone*. You felt like tearing the plywood off and letting light in. You thought that, maybe, that would kill the Mouth (or at least shut Him up).

You hadn't said anything. Just *thought* it. But the Great Dark Mouth replied anyway. He, like Mr. Suicide, could read your thoughts. "You don't want to kill me. I'm your savior, bucko. You *can't* kill me. I'm your god, bucko."

You wanted to scream back at Him, but realized that if you protested you'd be lying. He was right. Moreover, screaming would have been decidedly unwise. Already, you noticed a dude glaring at you. He was skinny and shirtless, with a long greasy salt-and-pepper mullet and heavy salt-and-pepper stubble. His teeth were clenched in an expression that spoke simultaneously of anger and bemusement.

What could you do? You ignored him. Tried (ridiculously) to pretend you were a member of the parade out on a wee merry stroll. That didn't work. The man knew better. He still glared. First he looked at your face and then his gaze lingered away from your face. Lowered. He must have been looking at your jeans. The blood from your leg wound was starting to stain them. You stopped and rolled up your pants leg. It was a small cut, in comparison to the one on your arm from the night before. You took off your backpack, rummaged around inside, and tied a white T-shirt around the outside of your jeans, at the location of the cut. Figured it would apply some pressure on it. Stop the bleeding. That helped, but it still hurt.

Mullet Man spoke to you. His voice was scratchy and gruff. "Hey kid, c'mere. I have a question for ya."

There is no honor among bums.

You kept walking and pretended you didn't hear him.

Mullet Man spoke up louder. "I need a place to stay, not all the time, I mean. Just at night and when it rains. You there all by yourself? Last year, I tried getting in there, but they had a security system all rigged up and I got tossed in the pokey for trespassing. That ain't right, you know. I mean, that ain't right, for you to have a place there when I found it first and had to spend time in the pokey because of it. I think I'm gonna have to pull seniority on you. I need a place to stay when it rains, or at night, or… hell, whenever I want to lay down."

Your brain was flooded by a million squishy-gushy thoughts. He wouldn't rest until you told him he could join you. And if you just shrugged and left, you felt certain he would enter the building and discover the body. Maybe you should invite him in, have him walk in first, and then tackle and stab him? You let the fantasy work through your brain, frame by frame, and found yourself enthralled by it and the freedom it represented. But then you envisioned the aftermath—the way the Mouth would laugh at you and declare that you once again succumbed to temptation. He would compare you to Dahmer and all His other failed disciples and scorn you for clinging to the first step of the Three-Fold Path and not exhibiting a willingness to move onto the second. Maybe then He would declare you a total reject and tell you to not even bother getting a passport. Certainly, He would call you a flesh-thing, and you'd come to realize what a scornful epithet that was meant to be.

You shrugged and left.

The Great Dark Mouth, for the first time, offered His congratulations. "Well done, my true and faithful servant. You have resisted a temptation. Now move on, bucko, and say no more to the moron across the street."

You did as He commanded because it felt good to have His approval. You felt ten pounds lighter when you paced away from there, not even answering Mullet Man's questions about who you were and where you came from and how you got that bloody mess all over you. (Oh yes, *that.* You'd forgotten that you must have looked like you'd just finished a day's work at a slaughterhouse.) Old instincts emerged, telling you to mentally beat yourself up over your carelessness. You shushed them, even though you knew you were as good as caught now.

Something about Mullet Man told you he wouldn't be willing or able to keep all of this to himself. Yeah, he was just another street idiot. But it didn't take Sherlock Holmes to attach a bloody dead body to a bloody man leaving the scene of the crime. None of this had happened yet, but you felt it—literally *felt* it—hanging in the air behind you. It was like there was a giant finger in the air that was about to flick over the first in a series of dominoes and each *click-click-click* of one falling after another brought you closer to the end—where the last falling domino would trigger a Rube Goldberg machine to lower a trap door and drop you from the gallows. Rube Goldberg machines being what they were, the hanging would be slightly botched and you'd suffocate slowly as people stared.

You'd liked to think of yourself as someone who wasn't easily rattled by cops or the threat of cops, but the truth of the matter was that if you'd been spotted like this—by a witness after a murder—a week ago or even a day ago you would've freaked. Would've pissed your pants and bawled like a baby. Shit, just look at the way you'd let Officer Douchebag Collins walk all over you.

But so much had changed. You'd heard—literally heard—your savior speak to you in both your waking state and in dreams. You now knew about the Three-Fold Path. If you were a normal person, just another marcher in the parade, you would have had great reason to worry about getting caught. But the Great Dark Mouth had spoken and made it clear that you had a way out. You would be able to escape your punishment because you would escape existence, itself. You were special. Set apart.

Chosen.

So you ignored Mullet Man and kept walking.

After a few moments, you could tell he'd regretted calling exclusive dibs on the place. He wanted company. He'd expected you to put up a fuss and try to broker some sort of homeless roommate situation with him (in the same way you'd tried to come to a similar understanding with the old man). He followed after you for about half a block, then gave up. About ten minutes later you heard a muffled scream.

He'd found the old man. So fucking what. You had more immediate concerns, like how badly you hurt.

Your stomach hurt with hunger, and your cuts hurt, and your heart ached from having to leave the old man behind, and your brain hurt from not yet being un-born, and your back hurt from having slept on the floor last night, and your feet (still) hurt from all the walking you'd done yesterday. Yet you trudged on. What kept you going, as you walked down the street, was the assurance that—after getting swallowed by the Mouth—you wouldn't hurt at all.

You attracted more stares. It was just like high school, the way people stared and gave you a wide berth. One lady—a fetching redhead in a short summer sundress; probably a cheerleader, about seven years ago—looked long and hard at you.

Redheads could be such *cunts*. You stopped walking so you could confront her. "Is there something wrong?"

She started to back away.

You walked closer. "I asked you a question, miss. The way you stared at me, it would seem that the mere *sight* of me offended you. Like you thought you were better than me. Like, maybe, you found something amiss. Could it be that I left my fly down?" You made an exaggerated gesture of checking. "Nope, that's not it. Hmm... I wonder... could it be that I have a booger hanging from my nose?" You wiped your bloody forearm along your nostrils, then looked to see if anything came loose. "Nope... it's not *that*. Could it be you're looking at some of the stains on my shirt and jeans... and... arm... and... well... face? Is that it, babe? Do I have stains on my face?"

She started to pace quickly away from you.

You giggled. "I was in a little tussle. A chivalric one, I can assure you. I was fighting to defend a girl's honor... for real, not *a girl*, really, but a *woman* who looked strikingly similar to you, actually. Except her legs weren't all skinny and tight and flawless like yours—they were, instead, horribly disfigured from an accident with her father's lawnmower when she was three. Y'ask me, though, that makes them all the sexier. I mean, no offense, but you're not mutilated enough to really turn me on. Anyway, some guy said she whored around all the time, and I told that guy he better shut up unless he wanted to get cut. If you think I look bad, you should see the other guy!" Then you started laughing. You made that whole thing up, right there on the spot. Did it seem plausible? Probably not, but it was sure worth saying, just to take a gander at her expression.

She turned her head. Looked concerned.

You were following her.

Her little pale freckled brow wrinkled. She bit her puffy lip, then started jogging away from you. Her little flower print sundress flittered up over her thighs with each step and you

thought about pursuing her—thought about *adding* the mu-
tilations Fate and Mother Nature had been cruel in depriv-
ing her—until you remembered the Mouth's admonition and
taunting.

Chastened by the memory (and worried that if you kept
talking to her, you'd no longer be able to control yourself),
you left. You shunned Step One to move along to Step Two.

There was a burger joint on the next block. It was breakfast,
so they weren't serving burgers. They were serving the breakfast equivalent of burgers. Sausage and egg sandwiches. But it
didn't smell like sausage or grease or egg or cheese in that place.
You instead smelled the overwhelming odor of melting wax.
It was coming from behind the counter. So-called sandwiches
made of wax were melting under the heat of lamps meant to
keep them warm until needed. It was like a toddler had taken
over, and tried to warm plastic play food with real ovens.

A plastic mannequin hand positioned itself at exactly the
right angle so it could pick up one of the sandwiches from
under a heat lamp. The plastic hand was attached to a plastic
arm, which was in turn attached (flimsily) to a plastic torso. Atop the plastic torso rested a plastic head, with molded
blonde plastic hair and blue plastic eyes. There was a hinge
in the mechanism that allowed part of the chin and mouth to
move (the same way the chin and mouth of a ventriloquist's
dummy moved).

"We need three more sausage and eggs," the goofy falsetto
voice exclaimed. It wasn't a woman's voice. It was a man's voice
providing a shoddy over-the-top imitation of a woman's voice.

Loony tunes.

Then the mannequin's plastic legs carried it to the orange
juice machine, where something the color of antifreeze leaked
out of a tap.

Batshit Loony Tunes.

None of the other wage slaves behind the counter seemed aware that their coworker wasn't human. None of the customers did, either. They didn't notice the fake cashier and they didn't notice the fake food. They tore their teeth into the wax and swallowed it down, hard. There was a steady din of wax-eating sounds in the dining area. You walked to the men's room, and felt grateful when the noise was dulled by the door.

You took a long look in the mirror. You'd only spent one day on the streets and, already, you looked transformed. Sure, you were caked with blood. But there was something else, too. It was like you'd aged a year in a day.

You checked the bathroom and confirmed there wasn't anyone else present. Then you looked back in the mirror. You smiled and then grimaced at the sight. "I'm a murderer," you said to yourself, in a voice that was barely a whisper. "I did it. Wow. I *did* it."

It was hard—both physically and mentally—to wash off the old man's blood. Hard, physically, because the bathroom had no paper towels. You had to grab handfuls of toilet paper and use it to scrub the red gunk away. When you scrubbed, your hands trembled. When you scrubbed, it irritated your scratches. Made them bleed again (and they'd started to heal). You applied pressure with some more t.p., and that seemed to work, but damn, it slowed you down when you didn't need to be slowed down.

It was hard, emotionally, because you felt like you were, in a sense, losing your trophy of the evening. You patted your pocket. You still had the knife. As long as you had that, you couldn't forget him.

A (non-plastic) man walked in when you were about two-thirds of the way through. Glanced over at you, sneered, and walked over to the urinal. You heard and smelled his rancid piss stream out. Ignored it as best you could and washed away the evidence. (Of course, you weren't really washing away the evidence. The blood that had been on your face wasn't eliminated, you'd just transferred it onto the sopping wet toilet tissue.)

The urinal dude didn't bother flushing but instead walked behind you, cleared his throat, and waited for you to vacate your place in front of the mirror and sink. You hastily finished wiping your face as clean as you could and dropped the toilet paper in a waiting trash can. You didn't have the presence of mind to take it with you into a stall and throw the goddamned toilet paper into the goddamned *toilet,* where you could flush it (and its DNA evidence) away. No, you were in a hurry, because urinal man wanted to wash his hands after handling his own dick. So you threw the t.p. in the trash.

You *did* go into a stall, though, eventually (to change clothes).

You *did* have the presence of mind to think it would be a poor decision to throw your bloody clothes in the trash, so you tucked them away in your backpack. But you *didn't* have the presence of mind to wait until urinal dude was done with the sink. If he paid any attention at all to you, he probably could tell what you were up to, in the stall. So, really, he was another witness.

You were collecting them that morning (witnesses, that is). You collected them the way pockets collect lint. Urinal Dude. Leggy Lady. Mullet Man. They could all attest to the blood stains on your face and your strange demeanor. They were three very different people, and yet—the moment the news of a murder downtown had been announced—they would all likely be calling the confidential police tip line. Ratting you out. Three very different dominoes. *Click-click-click.* Rube

Goldberg. The gallows.

"Stop wringing your hands, flesh-thing." The voice came from behind you. You couldn't speak to the Mouth, not with urinal dude rubbing his mitts over and over against the hot air of the electric hand dryer. So you went ahead and *thought* a reply, instead.

You talking to me or to urinal dude?

"Ha! You really think I'd consider *him* to be someone worth talking to? You gotta realize, I'm pretty select in who I hang out with. Only *fascinating* people draw my interest. Only *fascinating* people can hear my voice. I've had my eye on you for months now, bucko! When you banged and injured that retarded chick, I was pretty certain you were *fascinating* enough to chat with."

She wasn't *retarded. She just needed crutches and braces to get around.*

"Well excuuuussse me. I'll correct myself, in that case. When you banged *that cripple*, I was pretty certain you were fascinating enough to chat with. The point is: talking with me is a rare treat. You need to know that. Being *watched* by me isn't that big of a deal, mind you. I have *eyes* in every dark place—here on Earth and elsewhere. Every night sky. Every lightless room. Every shadow. Through those eyes, I observe billions. Being *heard* by me isn't that big a deal either. I have ears in every dark place, too.

"So I'm watching you and listening to you from the shadows, bucko. Every shadow in this bathroom. But I'm *speaking* to you from only one shadow. Your own. I only have one mouth. That I decided to bring it here, to Louisville, just to speak to you both in dreams and while awake is something you should consider an honor. So many want to be spoken to, and I can only take time to speak with one at a time. So many want to be devoured, and I can only devour one at a time.

"Likewise, you should consider it an honor to now start Step Two in the Three-Fold Path: Derealization. By allowing you to see the unreality of the people and places and things surrounding you, I've actually *sharpened* your senses, bucko. Where's the gratitude?"

So going nuts is a privilege?

"Why must you think things like that? You're not—as you've phrased it before, in your thoughts—'batshit loony tunes', at all! You're only a tad bit... nervous. That's all, bucko. Just a little on the jittery side. To say otherwise is blasphemy!"

Please understand, I don't want to be a blasphemer. It's just that... I've wanted to go mad for a very long time. My older brother went mad before me. My mother is a little wacked out, herself. Last night, I killed a man. Now I'm seeing plastic people and hearing voices. Are you telling me these things aren't related? What if I follow the Three-Fold Path and it doesn't work because it's only a delusion? What if I still exist *even after all of this?*

"Let me ask you this, bucko—do you think most lunatics *suspect* they're lunatics? Especially at the beginning, at the first onset of symptoms? Before someone has taken them aside to *tell them* they're a lunatic? I would go as far as to say that your suspicion that you're mentally ill is the best evidence available that you're *not* mentally ill, if you get my meaning. Stop being such a flesh-thingy worry wart!"

I'm not a worry wart! I guess you could just say that I'm... con-cerned. Don't you think, with all the attention I've attracted, that I have good reason to be... well... concerned.

"Not if you do what I tell you, bucko. Don't worry about the witnesses. No one can hurt you if there's no 'you' to hurt. So you better get your ass over to your mother's house and get that... pardon my language... mother*fucking* passport. Just keep your eyes on the prize. You're doing fine. I did mention to you earlier that I was damned proud of the way you didn't go all squishy-gushy on the guy outside of the dry cleaners this morning, didn't I? I mean, *damned* proud of you. That's all you should worry about, from here on out. My opinion of your progress should be the sole barometer of your self-esteem. And I do insist that you *progress* toward your destiny. After you leave this john, you're going to grab a bus home. Then you're going to walk into your mother's room and collect your passport."

That's another thing I've been meaning to ask you about. How can I collect the flesh or blood passport and avoid squishy-gushy?

"You'll know when you get there, bucko. You'll see *a sign* outside the house that will give you a tip for how things will go down. That's all I'll say for now. I want you to trust me, without knowing all the details. Blind faith is the purest form of submission. You'll know when you get there. Now, you're going to notice some police activity outside the restaurant. Your job is going to be to ignore that police activity and pretend like you're out on the proverbial wee merry stroll. You can do that, can't you? Your leg hasn't been so lacerated that you're crippled now, just like your ex?"

I checked it when I changed. It's not bleeding so much, anymore. I put a fresh T-shirt around the wound, though, because the other one was getting a little messy. Took the sock off my arm, you know, where it got cut? Looks like that cut's healing up okay, so I took it off.

"I see… well… I suppose that helps, *some*. It doesn't look normal for you to wear a bloody T-shirt around your leg, you know? Of course, it doesn't look normal for you to be wearing a *clean* T-shirt around your leg, either, but it's a hair more normal than the bloody one. And you want to look as normal as you can, bucko. Can you do that? I think, if only for a little bit, you can. Now, go ahead and take a wee merry stroll to the bus stop, then take the bus to your parents' house. And don't let yourself get squishy-gushy anywhere along the way, understand? Any more slips out of you, and I might decide you're no longer fascinating at all. I may decide that I won't deliver you into un-birth. I'll leave you to the flesh-things and their justice."

Dominoes. Rube Goldberg. Gallows. Fear. Pain.

"Indeed. Now, if you'll excuse me, I have another potential immigrant to connect with. A young Saudi dyke unhappy with her lot in life."

You going to send her all the way to Louisville to get to The Border Crossing, too?

"Ha! Now that's a provincial notion, if ever there was one! You think the Great Dark Mouth only operates a single Border Crossing, and that single Border Crossing is in Louisville Fucking Kentucky?" He giggled. "You have a lot to learn, bucko. There are Border Crossings all over the Earth. I'd explain it to you but I have to move along—and that means *you* have to move along, too. Just do what I suggested, go to your house, get your passport, avoid squishy-gushy and—I promise—you'll be fine."

When you walked out of the men's room, you noted that the menu had switched from sausage and egg biscuits to hamburgers. Plastic cups of antifreeze-looking orange juice were replaced with plastic cups of oil-looking pop. The mannequin behind the counter rocked on the heels of her feet, then let out a grotesque whistle and scrubbed the counter.

You averted your eyes from her and glanced at the dining area. It wasn't as full as it had been. The morning rush was over and the lunch rush hadn't yet begun. Just as the Great

Dark Mouth predicted, there were two uniformed cops out in front of the restaurant. They were taking statements from bums. When you walked out to the bus stop, one of them glanced over in your direction. You felt his eyes lingering over you. Got the feeling you were being assessed. You glanced back at him. Caught the expression on his face. He was staring at your backpack. You thought he was trying to sort out if you were homeless or a student. If the former, he'd want to interrogate you.

But the Mouth had spoken to you. ("... your job is going to be to ignore that police activity and pretend like you're out on the proverbial wee merry stroll. I know you can do that. Take a wee merry stroll to the bus stop and ride the bus to your parents' house.")

You still were not one hundred percent convinced you weren't going nuts. But you were comforted by the Mouth's observation that people who went nuts were not usually aware they were going nuts. You were comforted to have any direction at all. Ignore the cops, the Mouth said. Pretend like you're taking a wee merry stroll, the Mouth said. Above all else, don't worry, the Mouth said.

It was pleasant advice, and you needed some measure of pleasantness. So you did as the Great Dark Mouth told you. And if the cops still suspected you were homeless and/or had information to share about the atrocity reported to them, they didn't act on that suspicion. Maybe the Mouth knew what He was talking about. After all, you'd cleaned yourself up and changed your clothes, and they were looking for the blood-stained youth reported to them by Leggy Lady and Mullet Man. You were relatively calm, and they were most likely looking for someone who seemed unhinged. It probably didn't hurt that a group of Jefferson Community College students lingered near you at the bus stop, waiting to take the 17 back to the Highlands. You didn't exactly blend in with them, but you were young and they were young and you wore a backpack and they wore backpacks.

Now, that guy with the pants so raggy you could kind of see some of his dingy underwear, that guy with the beard down to his belly, *that* guy was homeless. Better to ask *that* dude about the goings-on in the neighborhood.

So you waited for the 23, because your passport was in Hikes Point. It came before the 17 arrived to pick up all the community college wannabe-hipsters. You wondered whether this, in a sense, outed you as an outsider. You weren't with that group of students. An observant cop would have picked up on that. But, lucky for you, the Louisville-Metro Police Department is not known for its cleverness. You got on the bus unmolested.

There was a disabled girl up front. She looked to be a couple of years older than you. She had big old tits—not firm, unfortunately, but humungous in a way that managed to escape sloppiness. She was wearing a white tank top that fit snugly around them. More importantly, she had the hottest legs you'd ever seen: skinny-scrawny, heavily scarred, and crumbled-up-looking. You suspected they'd been broken in several places, because they seemed to almost unfold—accordion-like—from her torso. But in that first, quick glance at them you weren't able to determine if the breaks were a result of her condition or of some surgical intervention to *address* her condition. They poked out of a denim skirt that rose to about an inch below the knee. They were alabaster with a tinge of pink around the ankle. They glistened. You guessed that they were sweaty but cold, the way Cressida's legs had been. Sweaty and cold and somehow sick. You tried not to stare at them too obviously. She might think you were gawking because you were disturbed by the sight of her. She might not get that you were just admiring her beauty.

The Great Dark Mouth had warned you not to engage in any squishy-gushy, but this was public transportation—possibly the least sexy locale in all of Louisville. Likewise, it was one of the less-promising venues to kill without detection. So there was no harm in having a closer look. And you had a plan to *get* a closer look.

XIV

You swung your backpack off your shoulder and pre-tended to drop it. It fell right next to her feet. She wore ratty tennis shoes. Once white, now dingy. Cracked leather. Frayed laces. But that's not what you were there to look at. You used the opportunity granted by your "accident" to get up close and personal with the legs. They smelled like suntan lotion. Maybe that's what made them glisten. Not sweat, but lotion. You started to daydream about putting lotion on those legs, but heard a guy behind you clear his throat, and you realized it was time to pick up your backpack and find a seat.

All the TARC buses had this big, empty area in front reserved for wheelchairs. That's where she sat—in that miniature wheelchair parking lot on the bus, right in front of the first row of seats for regular, non-deformed folks. You grabbed a seat in that front row and smiled and started making small talk.

"I can't believe I did that. My hands must have been sweaty. Just call me butterfingers. Damn this heat."

She looked at you. Craned her neck from one side to another. The skin of her neck looked so pale and soft, not scarred or even blemished. You ordinarily didn't succumb to traditional standards of beauty, but—on *her*—a soft, swan-shaped neck worked. You dug it. She took a deep breath in. Smiled softly. It looked to you like she was weighing her options, mulling over if it was wise to speak to you (and if it was, sorting out what her reply would be). It came out a little bland, for your taste: "I don't mind the heat so much."

Hardly a promising exchange… it didn't seem to indicate any potential for romance. But then again, you couldn't have a romance. The Great Dark Mouth prohibited it. If you tried to tap that, He would be through with you. Forever.

The Great Dark Mouth was a jealous god, demanding that you have no other gods—or goddesses—ahead of Him. But you weren't worshiping her, you were only *admiring* her. Making a little conversation. Killing time during the long bus ride.

"I'm heading back to my mom's house," you announced. "There's something… well… something for me to pick up there. I moved out the other day. Didn't pack everything I needed, though." You were telling her the truth… from a certain point of view.

You tried to make eye contact with her, but now *she* was staring at *your* leg. Or, more specifically, the T-shirt tourniquet *around* your leg. Little specks of blood started to leak through your jeans and onto the white cotton.

"A little young to be out on your own, aren't you?"

You bit your lip. "Naw, I'm eighteen now."

"I'm twenty-five," she said. "And I only got out on my own last year."

That surprised you. You knew she was a little bit older than you, but you didn't know she was *that much older.* You wracked your brain for a clever follow-up line, but nothing emerged. So you looked out the window and felt yourself tugged toward the side of the bus as it turned right onto Baxter Avenue.

"I waited until I'd saved up some money," she said. "And I

waited until I was in a good place in life." She looked at you with glassy blue eyes. "Are you in a good place in life?"

A couple of flies buzzed around your backpack, sensing the gore slathered across your old clothes but unable to get to it. You shooed them away. "I'm sittin' in air conditioning on a hot day," you said. "And sittin' next to a pretty girl. So I suppose you could say that's about as good a place as any." You didn't grin when you said this, because you didn't want her to think you were being sarcastic. But all your efforts at being a smooth operator were derailed by the unexpected nonsense that came out of her mouth next, like so much verbal diarrhea.

"When I asked you whether you were in a good place in life, I meant: do you know Jesus? Because the very best place of all is in His arms. That's what my pastor tells me, whenever I get to feeling sorry for myself for being in this chair. He says it makes no difference that I can't walk, because if I let Jesus carry me in His arms, I can go anywhere. Do you believe in Jesus?"

You tried, but couldn't keep from scowling. To say you felt disappointed would be an understatement. You felt as though you'd been sold a fraudulent set of goods. Those legs and those tits had "fuck me" written all over them, but you weren't two minutes into making your move before she dropped "Jesus" into the conversation. Beliefs that conventional had no business coexisting with a body so scantily clad and deliciously deformed. You didn't say anything. You were taken aback. You didn't want to offend her, so you paused. And when you paused, you considered fibbing and telling her that, hell yeah, you believed in Jesus. You believed in him so much, you wanted to hear her call out his name while she was on her back, legs spread for you. But you didn't say that. You just sat there, looking dumb.

"That's a no," she said. Then she grinned. She started wrig-

gling around in her chair. Lowered her head to start search-
ing through her purse. With her glance directed there, you
were able to get a nice glimpse of cleavage. You wanted to bite
off her breasts and fuck the wounds. You chastened yourself
for veering into squishy-gushy thoughts. *Flesh-thing*, you told
yourself. Flesh-*thing*. You felt disappointed (once more) when
she raised her head up and her eyes met yours again. She thrust
a little piece of paper toward you.

"My church asked me to write a gospel tract, with my testimony. It talks about how Jesus keeps me going. I'd like for you
to have it."

You didn't want to take it, but you didn't want to stop the
conversation. And you had enough experience with these kinds
of people to know that if you didn't take her tract, the conversation would be over. So you took it. In the end, you were glad
you took it, because it had a black and white picture of her on
the front page. She was all dolled up like she was on her way to
church. Wore a pretty skirt and top. More modest than what
she was wearing now. More formal, too. But it would still be
sufficient to jerk off to.

Squishy-gushy, you reminded yourself. None of that. Tran-
scend it all. You forced your eyes away from the picture.
"Thanks. I'll be reading it, I really will, because I think you're
a fascinating person and I want to know more about you."

When you said that, some redness crept into her ivory face.
She giggled. Oh, how you almost lost control and raped her
right then and there, when you heard that giggle! It was the
sort of giggle more appropriate for a girl-on-girl porno flick
than evangelism aboard a TARC bus. *No squishy-gushy*, you reminded yourself. But she was too damned perfect. The perfect
temptress, at least, for you.

Maybe the Great Dark Mouth had placed her in your path,

on purpose. There were shadows there, on the bus. Sun crept in through the windows, fell on passengers' noses, and formed shadows underneath them. So, the Mouth could be there, watching. Watching, literally right under your own nose! He must have given you this wheelchair-cutie as a temptation; as a way to test your devotion.

The one, true god—the Mouth—had placed a tool of the false god Christ in your midst as bait. You felt yourself getting hard. You told yourself it was just the motion of the bus. You'd heard that before, once. That certain kinds of transportation—buses and trains, primarily—could trigger an involuntary hard-on. You looked out the window and took a deep breath. *Down boy*, you thought. And it seemed to obey.

When she was finally through with her temptress-giggling, she asked you a question. "What is it about things that are so bad, right now, that you had to leave home? I mean, maybe I can help. Well, what I mean is, maybe I can't help—on my own. But maybe Jesus can help, *through me*. You mentioned you were going back to your mom's house. Is it your parents? Is that the problem? A lot of teens find it hard to submit to their parents' authority. But God's word says to honor your father and your mother, so what other choice is there? I mean, you have a choice. We're given free will. But what other *godly* choice is there?"

Talking to this girl made you miss Cressida more than you had in awhile. She might have been a little too fragile and a back-stabber, to boot. But at least she was under no delusion that her mother and father deserved *anyone's* fucking honor. "I see your point," you fibbed.

She saw through that, though. "I mean, it's not always easy. But that's kind of the point. Advancing in holiness isn't easy. If it was easy, then it wouldn't be so precious."

The bus stopped in front of Mid-City Mall and let on a few passengers. A black hippy chick, a white hippy chick, and one of the hairy, Bosnian immigrant dudes who'd been shipped to Louisville back in the '90s (you could tell because he was yammering away on his cell phone in some vaguely Eastern European language). The girl in the wheelchair kept on talking, but the Bosnian guy distracted you from what she had to say. He was fucking ugly, in a way that was fucking beautiful. All big, broad forehead and long, bony jaw. Decadent cheekbones that looked like tumors jutting from his emaciated frame. He squeezed in next to you, to your right, and kept on talking. He was wearing some shitty cologne that didn't cover up a heavy smell of cigarette smoke. That scent wafted alongside the lingering smell of the disabled girl's suntan lotion and now you could no longer restrain yourself. The boner happened.

You felt embarrassed that it happened. Felt relieved that your bigass backpack was on your lap and hid it. But then your remembered your gore-stained clothes were tucked away in that backpack, and that just made your boner all the fiercer. The old man's gore... *so close* to your cock.

"So, do you want to say it with me?"

The Bosnian guy kept talking on his cell phone, laughing every now and then.

"I'm sorry," you said, "I didn't hear everything you had to say there." You jerked your head in the direction of the chattering Bosnian.

"Do you want to say the Sinner's Prayer with me. Right here and now? What I guess I'm asking is, do you want to be saved?"

Salvation. What did that really mean? The Great Dark Mouth was offering you the closest thing to salvation you could imagine... *salvation* through *annihilation*. It required no prayer. And rather than insisting that you honor your mother and father, He told you to take some of your mother's bones or flesh or blood away from her as a passport. And yet, you suspected there was a thread of commonality between the two paths: both embraced self-denial. Maybe there was something you could learn from her.

"Before I answer that," you said, "I have a question *for you*."

"God's word says 'ask and it shall be given'. Better you ask Him the questions, than me. In prayer."

You gave her your hurt-little-boy look. It worked.

"Oh, I'm sorry… I didn't mean to be rude… What I meant was…"

"My question had to do with… well… how you do it?"

She squinted and cocked her head to the side, a gesture of confusion. It showed off that swan-neck again. You bit your lip. "How do I do what?" she asked.

"I mean, you said it isn't easy, being holy. What helps you with it? I guess you could say I'm looking for advice for fighting temptations."

"That's a good question to ask," she said. "I wished I'd asked that when I first got saved, because it would have prevented a lot of struggling. I was foolish then, you know. Thought that once I was saved I never had to worry about holiness ever again. What helps me is to remember that even though I have free will, I lovingly offer that free will up to the Lord. In that way, I become like unto a living sacrifice. And that's what He wants us to be. He wants us to willingly give up our will to His will. And if I'm living in God's will, then I know there's no way to fall to temptation, because the Lord is above and beyond all temptation. He proved that when Satan offered Him temptations in the desert. God's word talks all about that. That's what you should really do. Open up your Bible to… " She got out her smart phone and began typing. While her eyes were distracted, you gazed at her legs again. Smelled the lotion-cigarette-cologne scent again. Bit your lip. Felt your erection throbbing. "The Book of Matthew, chapter four, verses one through eleven. That's a good passage about temptation."

"I don't have a Bible."

She grinned and reached into her backpack. "You do now!" She handed you a slim New Testament. You went through the motions of looking up Matthew, chapter four. You put her gospel tract inside as a book marker.

"I know all about temptation," she said. "I have a cousin who tried to get me to drink alcohol once. But I told her I gave my will and my life up to the Lord, and that when that can of Budweiser was pushed my way, I didn't see a good time, I saw sin and I saw Satan. That's the real trick," she said. "You have to start to *see the world as your Lord and savior would have you see it*. If you see the world that way, then all those temptations will be rendered so unappealing that you won't have to worry."

And those words were like a magick spell. She spoke them and they slithered out of the air, into your ear, toward your brain then down into your optic nerves. For you realized, now, that she wasn't sent by the Great Dark Mouth to tempt you. Or, at least, not *just* to tempt you. You realized, now, that despite being caught up in a web of conventional delusions, she nonetheless was the inadvertent carrier of a certain wisdom.

A *very important* wisdom.

You knew it was dangerous to be stuck in Step One of the Three-Fold Path, and you were in danger of getting stuck there. The world was teeming with temptation, because the world was teeming with ugliness. An ugly river coursed through ugly towns, littered with ugly businesses and inhabited by ugly people who were hosts for ugly diseases and vehicles for ugly behavior. For you, the commonplace cancer patient was like a supermodel. X-rays of tumors were like centerfolds. Amputations were like orifices. Disease was an aphrodisiac. Advanced age was an aphrodisiac. Decay? An aphrodisiac. So you began muttering under your breath. You said a prayer to the Great Dark Mouth. Asked Him to give you the strength to push away from Step One and proceed to Step Two, where all temptation would be removed from you as you moved on to a state of total (not merely incidental) Derealization. And so your Lord and savior, the Mouth, heard this prayer. And He answered it. He was good—oh so good—to you. For, one moment you saw the most tempting piece of disabled ass ever sitting in front of you, crinkled-up accordion legs and all. The very next moment you saw an array of crudely-fashioned plastic limbs covered in a denim miniskirt. They were connected by squeaking pulleys and frayed rope to a plastic torso that wore a white tank top and a plastic head adorned with molded plastic hair and blue plastic eyes. There were two plastic mounds where breasts should have been, and they looked like the unmoving tits on a department store mannequin. The wheelchair was plastic, too. It looked like an oversize Fisher-Price toy.

You heard a cartoony voice next to you, and turned toward the Bosnian man. His ugly, broken features had been smoothed out—the extremes removed from them—as he, too, was revealed to be nothing more or less than a mannequin. A plastic man holding a plastic device, now revealed to be a toy cell phone. You could hear a voice coming out of it. It sounded like the teacher in Charlie Brown.

All the riders on the bus were now plastic.

You told the girl in the wheelchair that you were finished listening to her, and that she should go bother someone else. You pointed at the Bosnian guy and told her that he was a Muslim.

She didn't even wait until the guy was off the phone before her little plastic hand shoved a gospel tract in his face. He waved it off and she stifled herself until a new passenger would ascend the stairs up into the bus, on wobbly plastic limbs. Then she would make eye contact with them, try to get a conversation going. But all the new plastic people who got on waved her off, too.

"No thanks," they told her, "I'm already saved."

XV

You got off the bus in Hikes Point and started walking back to your subdivision. A rattling noise followed your every step. You looked behind you, expecting to find a snake or someone playing maracas. But there was, apparently, no explanation for the noise. It was a nagging mystery, but one you were able to shove out of your head as your neighborhood appeared to you as it never had before.

The Gift of Plastic-Vision didn't depart from you when you left the bus. All the cars looked like a toddler's toy cars. All the pedestrians looked like marionettes or mannequins or action figures. They clomped down the street with clumsy, exaggerated steps, as if being poorly manipulated by invisible strings. They spoke to each other in cartoony voices.

You looked up into the sky and noted that the sun, itself, was actually the headlight from a car (you could spot a hint of chrome around the edges). Birds were plastic. Alley cats, too.

This was Step Two.

The plasticness erased the ugliness (or, at the very least, minimized it; took its bite away). You supposed it could have been possible for the plastic features to appear to you as ugly features. Halloween masks were plastic, and they could boast facial features that were hideous or grotesque. But when you saw the plastic faces around you, you didn't see Halloween masks. You saw a sort of generically non-offensive array of facial features repeated over and over on various heads. Pleasant action figures. Pleasant dolls. Pleasant mannequins.

Many people would have experienced this new world as a hostile intrusion into their reality. But you'd been given enough information by the Mouth to be able to properly contextualize things. Seeing things as unreal didn't alarm you. It was a necessity; a step along the path to nonexistence. In a way—at least, at first—it comforted you. It relieved you from the burden of ugliness and verified that the magick of the Path worked.

But how to grab your passport? As you trudged along the sidewalk, you considered various ways you might be able to gather your mother's flesh or blood without resorting to squishy-gushy. You could put broken glass at the foot of her bed, so that when she woke up she'd cut herself. Then you'd collect a shard of glass with your mother's blood and... *voila*... instant passport. Or maybe you'd sneak a pair of scissors with you into her room and quickly snip off a tiny piece of earlobe. She'd wake of course. But by the time she knew what was happening, you'd already be out the door. That wouldn't count as squishy-gushy, would it?

Of course there was always the possibility that when you arrived at your house your parents and your brother would be plastic and fake, like everyone else.

You supposed that a plastic mother would make the passport collection process easier. But you also worried about what such a passport would look like, when presented to the bouncer at The Border Crossing. If you presented a plastic-looking finger to him would he declare it invalid because it was "fake, fake, fake"?

But the Mouth had told you to trust Him. (*You'll know when you get there, bucko. You'll see* a sign *outside the house that will give you a tip for how things will go down.)*

And the Mouth knew what the fuck He was talking about. When you were across the street from your house—*no not* your house, *your parents' house, your parents' house*—you saw it festooned with yellow police tape.

CRIME SCENE DO NOT ENTER.

The shit had hit the fan. Your stomach hit the street. Police don't put crime scene tape up if they're investigating something mundane, like truancy. No, something much, much more significant must've occurred. Something violent.

Your brother had warned you about this sort of thing, hadn't he? The night before you'd left, he'd spelled it out for you: "Haven't you considered how... well... *extreme* her reaction might be?"

And you hadn't. Not really. Your planning had been entirely selfish. You didn't care who ended up getting the lion's share of her wrath after you were gone. You figured that would be their problem. You had your own problems to attend to.

You tried to convince yourself that, even if you'd offered for your brother to join you in the escape, he wouldn't have taken you up on it. His spirit had already been too broken. He was a model inmate in your mother's prison.

Besides, even *if* he'd wanted to take you up on it, he'd have been too mentally unstable to follow through with things. How long would it have taken you to get him up out of your closet and packed and ready to go? How much noise would he have made while packing? How impractically would he have packed? (Would he have, for example, insisted on taking his baseball card album with him, along with his twenty-year-old catcher's mitt, and a dozen other sentimental items he wouldn't have had room for?) There's no way you could have pulled it off without waking your mother.

You tried to force your brain to focus on the logic of those arguments, but it wouldn't cooperate. Instead, various alarming scenes ignited in your imagination. You might have been granted the Gift of Plastic-Vision, but that didn't apply to your daydreams. (At least, not yet.)

And so you saw the whole scenario play out in your head, in all its grisliness; acted out in flesh and blood, not action figures and puppets. Mom shooting your brother's kneecaps out from under him with your father's shotgun, perhaps shouting Bible verses while she did so. Your brother bloodied, begging Mom for mercy. Your father hiding in his room, too gutless to even keep her from shooting their own son.

Yes, that could explain the police tape. It would make all the sense in the world. Mom didn't have enough self-awareness to blame herself for your departure, so she'd find a scapegoat instead. She'd blame your brother. Say that he'd seen it coming. The two of you talked, hadn't you? Sometimes even talked *behind her back*. Your brother had known you were leaving and hadn't tried to stop you—hell, hadn't even *reported the matter to her* so *she* could stop you. For that greatest of all disloyalties, she had no choice but to inflict severe punishment.

Or, maybe Mr. Suicide came for a visit right after you left. Maybe he convinced your brother that he'd better go ahead and off himself.

Yes, that could explain the police tape, too. Out of bitterness for not being Chosen, he would renounce the Great Dark Mouth. Then Mr. Suicide would convince him that without *you* in the house to absorb the worst portion of Mom's wrath, it would fall on *him* and he would find it unbearable.

Mr. Suicide would convince your brother to use some particularly baroque method to dispatch himself. Auto-erotic asphyxiation, maybe. The images flashed through your head: he'd be hanging from a rope in the closet. Since he was exceedingly quiet and often stayed in his room, Mom wouldn't even notice anything was amiss for several hours. Maybe even half a day. Maybe she wouldn't find him until it was time to hang up laundry. She'd march toward his closet, muttering some bitchy gripe or another, open the door, and then discover her son naked and dead. She'd see his dull eyes (like those of the dead Siamese twins in your dream), his face frozen mid-orgasm (like the meat hook people). She'd see those things and she'd scream and then she'd sit down and ponder whether or not she should call 911. (She wouldn't want to make a scene for the neighbors.) Maybe she would even leave him like that until dinner time, until your father would come home and notice something was amiss. Ultimately, he'd find out and then, for the first time, insist on putting his foot down.

Maybe that's what happened. All of it flashed through your head.

But best to not jump to conclusions. You'd find out soon enough. You investigated the property to see if there were any little blue coperoos lurking about. There weren't. The crime scene tape hung with too much slack to have been freshly applied. But then again, it wasn't completely fallen away, either. The house and its occupants were still surrounded by a cloud of police activity, but the cloud was looser rather than tighter.

But a cloud was still a cloud now, wasn't it? You still had clothes in your backpack, stained with the blood of the old man. It just wouldn't do to waltz in there with incriminating evidence strapped to your back. Especially since the bits of flesh caked onto the clothes were starting to take on an odor.

You looked to see if there was any sign of your family being there at the house. Lights were on, but that was a poor measure of whether or not anyone was home because your mother always insisted the lights be kept on during those rare occasions when no one was home. She was terrified of intruders. Thought that leaving the lights on would deter them. Likewise, it was impossible to tell if any cars were in the garage, as its door was closed.

You had to have faith in the Great Dark Mouth. ("You'll know when you get there, bucko.")

You turned around. You would return to grab the passport, but not before getting rid of the murder evidence in your backpack. You considered where you might be able to drop it without detection. Throwing the clothes away in the trash seemed like a poor idea, simply because—in their current state—they'd surely attract attention. Various images flashed through your head. Dropping them into a storm drain. (But at this time of day, that was far too public an escapade to undertake.) Another option: going to the Ohio and adding your clothes to the ugliness that already floated there. (Again, too public. The Ohio might be an ugly river but it was the only river in the area that was worth a damn. Therefore, it attracted a certain tourist element who convinced themselves it was something worth looking at. Both on the Indiana side and the Kentucky side, there were bars and restaurants positioned along the waterfront. Each year they held a fireworks extravaganza and military air show over it. It was a gathering place, teeming with frolickers out for a wee merry stroll. Frolickers who would be taken aback by the sight of a disheveled young man polluting their cherished landmark with bloody, sweaty clothes.)

You kept walking. Thinking. Walking. Thinking. The rattling noise with you, all the way, like the sound of a pesky metronome that couldn't be turned off. *Ca-chink, ca-chunk, ca-chink, ca-chunk.*

When you arrived out on the main stretch of road, outside of the subdivision, you spotted a plastic homeless dude assembled from dirty, chipped Lego pieces. He didn't look like he belonged there. He looked like he should have emigrated over The Border Crossing many years ago. You supposed you could've said he looked *fascinating*. He was thin and gaunt, (as thin and gaunt as you could imagine a Lego man being, at least). He was in the midst of quite an animated discussion with himself. He talked like Elmer Fudd. When he saw you coming, he stopped talking and smirked. Pulled a rubbery, white-gloved hand up to his face. Put a rubbery, white-gloved finger up to his lips. Shushed you.

He was the one talking to himself, and *he* shushed *you*.

You giggled.

"Be vewwy, vewwy quiet," Lego Homeless Man said. "I'm hunting aliens."

Lego Homeless Man was clearly a lunatic, and this troubled you (but not for the usual reasons people are troubled by lunatics).

You and the Great Dark Mouth had talked about schizophrenia, and He'd convinced you that you were not mentally ill. But in the back of your mind you'd still wondered. You considered the possibility that sanity and insanity were still two valid landmarks by which you could judge how your life was proceeding. Now a *lunatic* appeared fake to you. The concrete, objective existence of lunacy was essential; for we can only measure sanity by the presence or absence of *aberration*. When the *aberration, itself,* looked and sounded unreal, you realized such landmarks were useless.

But then again, hadn't the Mouth told you this? He'd said that *He* was to become the sole landmark of your life—that all other landmarks were useless. ("That's all you should worry about, from here on out. My opinion of your progress should be the sole barometer of your self-esteem. And I do insist that you *progress* toward your destiny.")

Was it possible to use Lego Homeless Man to reach your destiny? You felt the straps of your backpack chafe against you. *Yes,* you decided. *He could, in fact, be useful.*

"How *very fortunate* that you're hunting aliens," you told him. "I happen to be an alien hunter, too. As a matter of fact, I slew one just the other day."

"How do you know he's weally dead? They come back if yewuh not cewful," Lego Homeless Man said. He glanced to one side of the street, then another, confirming no one was eavesdropping. It was as though he was about to speak of privileged information that he was only sharing with you because you had the right security clearance. "Dey wessurwect on Sundays," he whispered. "I never killed one all da way. Dey always get back up." Then he let out a Fudd-like laugh. "Heh-heh-heh-heh-heh-heh."

You glanced around. None of the passers-by diverted their eyes from their wee merry strolls long enough to pay you any attention. If you were noticed at all, the two of you were simply dismissed as two chattering street people. So you felt safe taking a tiny risk. You took off your backpack. Unzipped it. Said to Lego Homeless Man, "Take a look in here, you'll see proof." You showed him the bloody clothes. Through the filter of Plastic-Vision, they appeared to be made out of vinyl and smeared with ketchup.

He looked at them and looked at them. You felt uncomfortable with such a long pause. When he finally glanced back up, he rolled his eyes at you. "Not at all impwessive! That's not alien blood. That's fwom a puwson! Alien blood isn't wed. It's gween! I found that out fwom Staw Tweck."

"Star Trek isn't real," you said (as though you, of all people, were now in a position to be arbiter of what was real and what wasn't).

Lego Homeless Man started to show signs of agitation; raised his voice: "I saw it on TV. And the camewa doesn't lie!"

Just then, a passing G.I. Joe-style action figure man turned his head to glare at you. There was a National Guard base nearby, and it seemed like he was taking a break from his chores there. (Although that made little sense—did military people have "breaks" in the same way kids working at McDonald's did? Fifteen minutes and then back in the tank?)

In any event, he walked along the sidewalk with a stop-motion animation style that resembled a confident, heroic strut. He'd probably just returned from Afghanistan, where he'd been fighting for your freedom. If he went to the cops with suspicions that you were up to no good, they'd likely believe him. In popular opinion, a hero—like a camera—doesn't lie.

This was going to be harder than you'd imagined. You had to think fast. You lowered your voice to a whisper. "Be very, very quiet," you said. "The government is staring at us." You jerked your head in the direction of the G.I. Joe man.

Lego Homeless Man turned his head and saw the soldier. "Oh shit," he said. "I'm sowwy. I'll shush. I'll shush."

"You *better* shush," you said. "Or else he'll ship both of us off to Guantanamo. You know the government is in cahoots with them, don't you? The aliens, I mean. Down there, the aliens run the show. They put the prison down there, away from the U.S., so they can walk around undisguised."

"Weally? Gosh, I didn't know *that*. I mean, it's vewy believable. But no one told me that, befowuh."

This was the opening you needed. "You *didn't* even know *that*? Ha! Some alien hunter *you* are. My guess is that you're a mere rookie. Say, how long have you been at it, anyway?"

Lego Homeless Man stroked his face thoughtfully. "Five yeaws, maybe six. Maybe sixteen or six hundwed. I think six is in there, somewhewe."

"Well, *I've* been hunting aliens longer than that. Seven or seventeen or seven hundred years. And so I know a few things you don't. For example: the aliens sometimes drink red paint so that their blood looks red instead of green. How else do you think they've been able to walk amongst us for so long, undetected?"

"For weal?"

"Yes, for real."

Lego Homeless Man examined the contents of the bag once more. "So that all came fwom a dead alien? How did you kill him so that he didn't wessurwect?"

Ah, this was too easy. He was playing into your hands. You pulled out the knife that had belonged to the old man. "I used this. You see how the blade is silver?"

(It was steel, not silver, but Lego Homeless Man nodded his chipped plastic head in agreement.)

"Well," you said, "that's how I was able to kill him. This is a magic knife. If you stab them with *this*, they won't resurrect. It was handed down to me from the alien hunter who trained me. And I'm so very sad, because now I'm about to retire from alien hunting. I've seen too much death, you know. I'm sort of shell-shocked by the whole thing. So I'm about to leave the profession, and I have no one to give this knife to."

Lego Homeless Man scratched his head. "What do you mean, you wascally wabbit! I just told you I'm an alien hunter, too."

You gasped, as though surprised. "Well I'll be... That's *right*. You *have* just told me that! Would you, by any chance, be interested in carrying on the good fight with this weapon?" You cupped your hand around the knife, so passers-by wouldn't notice it.

"Boy would I!"

You slipped the knife into his hand. There was a flicker on and around his Lego face, and then you noticed the markings on it changed from those which portrayed a scowl to those which portrayed a grin.

"If you're going to take the knife," you said, "you're probably going to want my backpack, too. I mean, so you can sniff the clothes. Get a sense of what their blood smells like. Every hunter needs to know the scent of his prey." You slipped off the backpack. Held it out for him.

When he took it from you, he took on all your fears. The evidence was on him, not you. When he eventually had a run-in with the little blue coperoos (which, given his demeanor, he most likely would) they'd search him and find evidence of murder. They'd find DNA matching that of another homeless man. Assumptions would be made. Bum fights envisioned. Then they'd arrest him, and—despite idealistic notions to the contrary—a jury would deem him guilty until proven innocent. Most likely, he'd end up in a Lego Insane Asylum, attended to by Lego Nurses with Lego needles that would puncture his plastic and dope him up with happy-sleepy juice for the rest of his life.

Thinking through the whole scenario made regret spew through your brain. After everything you'd done—more or less without remorse—you were surprised you still had anything even vaguely resembling a conscience. The last time you'd felt anything like this, you'd just shot cum on the old man's face. But even *that* hadn't stopped you from plunging with him down even more exotic depths of squishy-gushy. Perhaps you felt regret because you realized you'd come to embody the old man's saying: "There is no honor among bums." Perhaps you felt regret because it was almost too easy. Lego Homeless Man had so very much wanted to believe in aliens and alien hunters, and your words provided an excuse for him to keep on believing in such things. If it had been harder, you'd have had more of a sense of accomplishment.

You felt a need to be extra-kind to him, as you said your goodbyes. You shook his hand in a pantomime of gregariousness and good cheer. "Best of luck, Alien Hunter, and thank you for your service to our country."

G.I. Joe Man was almost a block away when you said that, but you thought you spied his head turn ever so slightly toward you—as though he caught on to what you were saying and somehow thought you were talking about him. Perhaps he was ultra-alert to expressions of gratitude for service to the country. Maybe he had special sensors in his ears, designed to pick up such expressions so he could automatically respond to them. In any event, when it became clear you were talking to the homeless guy, G.I. Joe Man shook his head (stop-motion animation style). Even the briefest, most superficial experience with you had left G.I. Joe Man disgusted. He marched along, back in the direction of the National Guard.

You marched along behind him in the same direction (because Mom and Dad's house was only three blocks away from the National Guard armory). G.I. Joe Man marched back to his esteemed place on the ladder, where he fought for your freedom.

You marched toward your passport. Toward *true* freedom.

Ca-chink, ca-chunk, ca-chink, ca-chunk.

XVI

The night you'd turned eighteen, you'd had to sneak out like a thief in the night. But you didn't have to sneak back in. Shedding the backpack and the knife led you to shed fears of becoming a suspect. Who cared if cops were on the scene? As long as you weren't carrying evidence with you, you were good to go. You could simply present yourself before your parents and get your passport.

You still didn't know *how* you would get it, but the Great Dark Mouth had assured you that it wouldn't be such a difficult task.

You had faith in the Great Dark Mouth.

There would be questions, of course. Mom would scream at you. Try to slap you. Make you feel guilty. Try to convince you to stay. It was difficult to approach the house, knowing you'd be exposing yourself to all that when you walked in. But you would force yourself to tolerate that nonsense for the sake of the greater goal.

If you were lucky, it would be the last time you would ever have to interact with *any* ladder person, ever again. You'd get your passport, take a bus back to The Border Crossing and proceed to oblivion.

The yellow police tape still fluttered in the breeze. But now, it seemed as though someone was home. You saw silhouettes passing behind the window. Then you saw a plastic mannequin hand pull at the drapes. You saw the plastic shape of a young, Caucasian man with molded plastic brown hair.

Your brother. At least he wasn't hurt. (Though seeing him as a mannequin made you cringe.)

It seemed as though he saw you, as well. In fact, he jumped in an exaggerated manner (more like a marionette, than a mannequin) when he saw you. Through the thin walls of the pre-fab house, you could hear a Porky Pig style stuttering. Then the door opened. Your father stood there, trembling. He appeared to you as a pink rag doll, tattered and frayed. His head was adorned with alternating loops of black and gray yarn. Your stomach sank.

You didn't, yet, see your mother.

You bent down to slip past the crime scene tape. Your rag doll father was visibly shaking with your every step forward. You barely noticed the plastic stairs' familiar shift away from the foundation as you ascended them.

Your father closed the door.

You opened it.

Your father shrieked. Cocked his head toward your brother. Spoke to him in a voice not unlike that of Foghorn Leghorn. "I say, I say, I say, give me my bow and arrow, son."

"R-ree-r-ree-r-ree-right away, d-dee-d-dee-d-dee Dad!" Off he clomped to the garage.

"What's going on? Where's Mom?"

He ran a stuffed cotton hand over his yarn-hair. "I say, I say, you know full well where your momma's at, boy-ah! And now, I say, now you've come to do the same to us, haven't you?"

Your brother clomped his plastic legs back over toward your dad and gave him the archery equipment. Your father tried loading the arrow into the bow, but his cloth hands had no fingers. "Damned, I say, damned arthritis." Then he commanded your brother to call the police. "Tell Officer Collins that he, I say, he returned to the scene of the crime!"

"What crime?"

Your brother spoke up. His eyes were dull and lifeless, but somehow you had a sense he was glaring at you. "I *kn-knew* you w-were g-g-gonna try it," he said, in his Porky Pig voice. "You were trying to k-kill our m-mother, that dee-dee-day in the bathroom. And the n-night you left the h-house, you *dee-did* kill her. You dee-dee-dee-dee-dee-dee-*did*!"

This was some seriously fucked up shit.

Dad thrust his hand out toward you, as though trying to point. But, lacking fingers, it was a hollow gesture. "I say, I say, you even left a note claiming responsibility. I say, a note taunting the police. 'Don't look for me. You'll never find me.' Ha! Well, here we done found you all right! Found you, comin' right back to where you did the killin'! I reckon you must've gotten hungry out there. Decided to come back here and beg for some sort of mercy or leniency or somethin'. I say, boy-ah, I cain't figure you out at all. You is, I say, you is nuttier than a squirrel turd."

You heard sirens approaching.

"I didn't kill Mom!"

"They found, I say, they found your fingerprints on my shotgun. And that's how she done kicked the bucket, son. We cain't, I say, we cain't even go back to the garage, because, I say, there's blood still splattered out there where you shot her. How could you do this to me, knowin'... I say... knowin' that I was the one who found my own mother dead? And now, I say, and now... this." With that, Dad started sobbing. Instead of tears, thin, frayed strings started falling from his button eyes.

"This is fucked up. You guys think I killed her? I didn't."

Then you remembered a bit of conversation: "You wouldn't bat an eyelash if a certain M-O-M did herself in."

"Let me ask you. Didn't they find her prints on the gun, too?"

Dad cleared his throat. Batted tear-strings out of his eyes. They drifted down to the floor. "Why, I say, of course they did, son. We all reckon that's 'cause she was strugglin' with you. And if you don't mind me sayin', I reckon, I say, I reckon you look like you've been through a tussle or two since I last seen you, boy-ah. Why, you can even, I say, even see where her nails must've raked your face as she struggled for her life!"

"*She* didn't rake my face! Look, you've got this all wrong. Didn't they even consider the obvious... I mean, didn't they do ballistics to determine which angle the bullet came from? Didn't they see the powder burns on her hands?"

Your Rag Doll Dad shook from head to foot. "I say, I say, what you drivin' at boy-ah?"

"*She killed herself!* You don't get it, do you? She was nuts and she was miserable and the only thing she had was us, and when one of us left she couldn't handle it anymore and she finally listened to Mr. Suicide! He spoke to her and she finally said yes to him!"

Your father threw down the bow and arrow and started pelting you across the face with his stub-like, pillowy arms. "You is, I say, you is goin' to *Hell* for lyin', boy-ah! How dare you slander, I say, slander her memory! Your mother was a good Christian woman. Read the Bible more than anyone I knew. She wouldn't commit that ultimate sin! Iffin', I say, iffin' that's the story you're plannin' to try to tell the police, then I reckon, I say, I reckon you *belong* in the hoosegow! Iffin', I say, iffin' you want to run her reputation through the mud after you done murdered her, then I reckon you is no longer my son!"

"You know, that's the good thing about being dead, I suppose," your mother had told you. *"No one can run you into the mud anymore, on account of it's considered impolite."*

You turned toward your mannequin-brother. "But *you* remember… don't you remember? We talked about Mr. Suicide. You, yourself, told me you were worried about how *extreme* her reaction would be, if I left. You must have seen this coming! We talked about how Mom and Dad could probably hear Mr. Suicide talking, but pretended that they couldn't."

You cringed when he shook his head. "I dee-dee-don't know wh-what you're talking about! You k-k-killed her, and now the cops are gonna come and t-t-t-take you away!"

And that's when you realized the terrible truth. Your brother, too, had gotten good at pretending. Your mother was dead, and with the highest rung of the ladder now empty there was an ascension through the ranks. Your father was now at the top of the hierarchy, and *his* opinions now shaped the official version of reality in the household. And your brother moved up one step. Now *he* took your father's place as co-conspirator to deny what was going on. He now was in cahoots with the conspiracy to look the other way, to pretend. Maybe he did this due to sour grapes for not being deemed *fascinating* enough for anything other than messenger duty for the Great Dark Mouth. Maybe he did this out of simple, dumb reflex. But whatever the cause, he was doing it. And this betrayal—the cruelest betrayal, not only a betrayal against you but also against *truth*—almost made you cry, right there.

The sirens got louder.

You sprinted past your brother, toward the garage. Turned on the lights. Two brightly painted wooden trucks (like those found in a toddler's toy chest, only life-size) rested there. It took you a minute or two to find the spot where she'd done it.

The stains were still on the white plastic door. They looked like dried ketchup. You walked toward them. Licked your palm. It smelled funny and tasted funny. But when you slathered it over the dried blood it took on a heavy red tinge and that made you smile: you finally had your passport. Now all you had to do was get to The Border Crossing.

The sirens now blared. Car doors opened and shut. You heard Foghorn Leghorn whisper to Porky Pig, who then whispered something to a man who sounded like Chief Wiggum from the Simpsons. "C'mon out of the garage, loony! You're surrounded, nyah!" the Wiggum-voice said. "Come out, with your hands up!"

You looked out a window. Saw at least a dozen Tonka cop cars. Fell to your knees. Prayed to the Great Dark Mouth. "Help me... Help me get out of this."

He didn't answer. You knew that—from the garage's shadows—He saw and heard you. But His mouth was elsewhere, attending to the needs of His other charges. Perhaps He was busy helping the Arab girl who wanted to achieve communion with Him, too. He'd spared as much time as He could for you, that day. You should have, indeed, realized at the time just what an honor He'd paid you simply by acknowledging you.

There was a six-foot-tall metal cabinet where your father had kept saws and hammers and wrenches. You opened it. The tools, too, were all plastic now. Large enough to be used by an adult, but otherwise looking like something out of a little boy's toy tool chest. You threw some of them out so you would fit inside. They made scraping noises as they fell onto the gray plastic floor. You kept a hacksaw in your hand, though, for self-defense. Yes, it was plastic—but so were your assailants (and their weapons). At worst, the plastic saw would prove as ineffective as a toy. At best, you'd be bringing a saw to a gun fight.

Either way, wielding it was an absurdity. And yet, it felt better to hold on to it than to let it go.

You closed the door. It was a tight fit. Smelled of old oil. There were thin horizontal slits in the metal. They were your gills as your head swam in darkness.

The beauty of the blackness relaxed you. You decided to play a game. "I don't exist," you whispered to yourself. "I don't exist. This cabinet doesn't exist. This oil smell doesn't exist. They'll open this cabinet and won't find me because I won't exist. I won't exist. I don't need to go to The Border Crossing, because by sheer force of mind, I'll make it so I don't exist."

A long time went by. You heard the whir of remote control helicopters overhead. You heard cartoon voices in all directions demanding you "give yourself up." You chuckled. Little did they know that was the *whole fucking point*: to *give up* your very existence! You tried to block out all the voices. You were some-what successful. In time, they all sounded like the murmur in-side a sea shell. "They don't exist," you whispered. "I don't exist. None of this matters. None of this is happening."

You repeated such words (or similar ones) for a long time, and had almost succeeded in convincing yourself this was the case, when you heard the crashing of glass and a strange hissing. Moments later, all the doors came crashing down. You trem-bled. Heavy boots slapped against the garage floor.

"Don't exist... I don't exist... They'll open this door and won't see me here because I'll simply wish myself into *nonexiste*—"

And then the cabinet door was flung open, and there was light—terrible, eye-aching light. There was light shining from the fluorescent fixtures attached to the ceiling, making you wince. There were puffy red cotton balls blowing through the air—tear gas. It wasn't real, but it made you choke. Wheeze.

Their weapons could have a real effect on you.

A Fisher-Price policeman wearing riot gear, complete with gas mask, stood in front of you. You read the name tag on his uniform: D. Collins. Officer Douchebag Collins. He held his sidearm in his right hand. With his left, he turned on a long, thick black metal flashlight and shined it in your eyes. Not even an inch of shadow remained to hide in.

He spoke (in a muffled voice, through his gas mask) like Yosemite Sam. "All right, you lily-livered, pencil-necked varmint! I'm the rootinest-tootinest, hombre-shootinest policeman this side of the Pecos! Put down that thar weapon and get your belly on the ground like the worm you are!"

You stood your ground. Weren't about to surrender when you were so close to oblivion. You especially weren't gonna surrender to fuckin' Douchebag Collins. You spied a pale sweet spot of plastic skin in between Officer Douchebag's chest armor and helmet chin strap. You could aim the saw there and slaughter yourself a filthy little plastic pig.

But that would be squishy-gushy. The Mouth would not approve. You still had faith He would save you, as soon as He had time.

But you were so fucking tempted.

You flung down the hacksaw. Put your hands up. Then you heard a voice. You turned to meet it. A quartet of Weeble police officers rocked in place. One of them spoke (through his gas mask) with the high, nasally voice of Inspector Gadget: "Go, go gadget taser!" He shot the device and wobbled from the recoil.

And then there were two jolts, and there was shaking, and there were handcuffs. They'd caught you literally red-handed.

XVII

How can you describe the months that followed—
months stuck on the border between the final two
steps of the Three-Fold Path?

It was like rutting while on the verge of orgasm, but never
being able to come. Derealization was only ever intended to be
a way station, not a destination. You knew you weren't crazy,
but the Gift of Plastic-Vision might eventually *drive* you crazy.
Strangeness was only palatable in small doses. Given enough
time it became a sort of cluttered, disjointed ugliness all its
own. A kind of ugliness that didn't seem the slightest bit sexy.

And yet, the Great Dark Mouth saw fit to maroon you there
while He, presumably, helped someone else.

You ping-ponged between cartoony courtrooms with plush,
Cabbage Patch Kid-style bailiffs and cartoony jail cells with
bizarre Japanimation cell mates. You inhabited a Roger Rabbit
world that lasted ninety days instead of ninety minutes. The
worst part was when you looked at the reflective metal surface
bolted to your wall. (The jail gave you that instead of a glass
mirror because they didn't want you to break the glass and
make it into a weapon.)

When you looked at yourself, you realized that you, too,
were plastic. You screamed when you realized that. You felt

foolish, after screaming. Why should the sight of yourself be exempt from the Gift of Plastic-Vision? And yet, the reality of your unreality struck you as a nightmare. You were a plastic dummy (like your brother), with yarn for hair (like your father) and vinyl clothes. The only relief (if it could be called that) is that you now understood where the rattling noise came from—behind your plastic glasses, you had a cartoonish mad man's googly eyes. They rattled when you moved.

Ca-chink, ca-chunk, ca-chink, ca-chunk.

Why hadn't you figured it out? The old man—himself a pilgrim stuck at Step Two—had even made mention of your googly eyes. But you'd paid him no mind. Hadn't put two and two together. You'd been so foolish.

***

You, like everything else, were tangible. But you, like everything else, weren't real. Honestly, it was getting to the point where you began to experience the nagging desire to once again look real. You felt ashamed as this blasphemy began to assert itself in your plastic brain. Yet it was there. Each passing day you whispered prayers to the Great Dark Mouth, begging for help so you could move on to Step Three. Each passing day, the Mouth ignored you. Each passing day, the notion of going back to the way things were before you'd ever heard of the Mouth seemed preferable to this place (this location, yes, but also this *mental* place) where you'd arrived.

You resorted to absurd hijinks to distract yourself from your dilemma. The judge was a fat Arab who appeared to you—through the filter of Plastic-Vision—as Mr. Potato Head. Once, when you didn't like what he said, you got loose from the correctional officers and tried removing his mouth. It almost worked, too. You felt it give. If it hadn't been jammed in there so tightly, you would have succeeded. That would have been a hoot. You couldn't imagine what the court's reaction would have been if the judge had suddenly (and to them, in-explicably) turned mute.

But as you struggled to pry the mouth from that six-foot-tall Potato Head, bailiffs and correctional officers fell on you. They had numbers on their side. Governments on their side. The whole fucking *ladder* on their side.

Your disruptions made an impression. The judge deemed you incompetent to stand trial. He felt you were crazy. So cra-zy, you wouldn't understand the proceedings. You wanted to explain it all to him. Maybe fire your public defender. Repre-sent yourself. Demand to subpoena *Perfect Monsters* and admit it into evidence as defense Exhibit A.

(Where had it gone? It had been in your backpack. You'd given it to the Lego Homeless Man. All you'd have to do is serve a subpoena on Lego Homeless Man. It would've been simple. So damned simple.)

These were the thoughts going through your head the after-noon that the judge decided you should go to a funny farm for a spell. "Just until he thinks you're fit to stand trial, bro," your lawyer (a Ken doll) emphasized afterward. He had the accent of a Southern California surfer, but at the same time managed to sound condescending. He used a speak-gently-and-slowly-to-the-lunatic voice. Then he grabbed one of your cuffed hands and gave it a cold, plastic shake.

Your lawyer disgusted you, and so you felt relieved when a clanging, scraping noise broke through the din of the court-room and distracted your attention from him. A smiling statue of the Virgin Mary pushed itself across the polished plastic floor. You couldn't see its legs underneath the blue and white robes. It seemed to amble toward you on heavy, metal crutches.

It called out your name in a voice that sounded like Betty Boop's. It looked and sounded happy to see you. Looked and sounded happy, *in general.* You couldn't remember the last time anyone looked and sounded happy to see you. You couldn't remember the last time anyone looked happy, in general.

You'd heard a voice that had sounded kind of like Betty Boop's before, but couldn't quite place it.

The correctional officers carted you away before the statue could reach you.

The last thing you noticed about the Virgin Mary was that her belly was round with child.

***

They didn't take you straight to the funny farm. You cooled your heels in your jail cell for a few hours until they completed paperwork for your transfer. Your cell mate (a Japanimation race car driver) was sleeping. You're embarrassed to admit that it was only then, when you had time to think, that the true identity of the crippled Virgin Mary dawned on you. And with the recognition came a deeper resolve. *I must go back to seeing things the way I did before. I've been abandoned by the Mouth. I can't continue like this. I would have liked to seen her—really seen her.*

XVIII

Once upon a time you'd actually wished you were in the loony bin. You'd thought that you'd have rubber walls to bounce off of, and they'd be a comfort. That wish (like many of your wishes) had proven foolish.

The ugly truth was, the nuthouse wasn't all that different from the jailhouse. In some ways, it was worse. The plastic pills, for example. You weren't insane, so the meds had no impact on the way you thought or saw the world around you. But they put you to sleep. Also, you never saw any rubber walls in the nuthouse. If they'd had them, you wouldn't have had the energy to bounce off them.

When you exercised your right to refuse medicine, the Potato Head judge signed a court order robbing you of that right. Then action figure orderlies held you down while Fisher-Price nurses started giving you shots instead of pills, because they didn't want you hiding pills in your cheeks or under your pink plastic tongue. When the needles pierced your plastic skin, it didn't hurt as much as when you saw yourself as flesh. That, at least, provided some small comfort.

But the shots made you so tired, so out of it, that your memory of Our Lady of the Courtroom became foggier and foggier. You started to doubt yourself. You started to wonder if she'd been a dream.

Then one day, Public Defender Ken showed up at the nut-house to confer with you on legal strategy. He confirmed Our Lady of the Courtroom hadn't been a dream.

He usually sat across the table from you but this time he sat right next to you. Looked into your eyes for several seconds before starting to speak to you in that annoying surfer voice. "Bro—I've been contacted by a young woman named Cressida Petridis. That name ring a bell?"

You nodded.

Public Defender Ken slapped his plastic arm over your shoulder. "Well… I don't know how to say this because… yikes, dude, this is *intense*… she says that she's pregnant and you're the dahd. I mean, is that even possible? Did you do the deed with her?"

You nodded.

"Woah… Intense!" Public Defender Ken said. "Give me a fist bump, bro!"

You let out a stupid, sedated laugh. "A what?" you groaned. Of course, you knew what a fist bump was, but you were in-credulous. You hadn't expected to receive an invitation to fist bump from your public defender, even if he was a Ken doll.

Public Defender Ken took your plastic hand and raised it in the air with his. "Now make a fist."

You humored him.

Then *he* made a fist and bumped his fist against yours. "Re-spect, bro. Respect. This is the first good news for your case in a long time. A jury's gonna have to have mighty big cojones to sentence a new father to death. Especially when the new mother is disabled and seems like she's on our side. If you ever become well enough to stand trial, I'd like for her to testify. Dude, if she sheds tears on the stand on your behalf, then all the bitches in the jury will *totes* be on your side! She'll tell a different story about you than the one the media is telling. She can tell them that you were loving and sensitive. Just confused, that's all. Sick. But loving. Not an irredeemable psycho, but a confused kid who should have gotten mental health treatment years before. And who, despite being mentally ill, was once capable of great kindness towards a disabled girl. Fell in love with her. And therefore, doesn't deserve to die."

From the shadows under the table, you heard a giggle. Then another giggle. Then a snarky insult: "Flesh thing. Flesh *thing*! Oh yes, how *kind* you were to her, bucko. How loving. Oh yes, your motives were so noble. Not at all squishy-gushy! I wonder if her mother would want to testify, too? Talk about those scars and bruises she saw."

You poked your head under the table. "Where were you when I was surrounded by cops?" you sleepily asked the Great Dark Mouth.

"Beg pardon, bro?" the oblivious Ken doll asked. "Who are you talking to? Is there a midget under the table?" He let out a series of nervous giggles. Then a worried look besmirched his handsome, tan face. "Aw, man… For a while there, when I first started talking to you… You seemed a little less… ill."

How could he have arrived at that conclusion? You'd barely said a word to him before talking to the Great Dark Mouth under the table. Maybe that was the point. To the Ken doll, sanity equaled sedated silence.

"Looks like that pesky psychosis is starting to return, bro. I'm gonna get ready to head out so you can get some more medication."

"No more medication," you mumbled drowsily.

"If you want any chance of ever seeing that kid of yours, even if it's just in a prison visiting area, then I suggest you go ahead and take it. They aren't going to let someone who's actively psychotic around a rug rat."

Your plastic attorney had told you many things during your consultations. Things you thought were, for the most part, unhelpful to the point of being ridiculous. He'd told you to sit straight in court instead of slouching, for example. He'd said that would make a better impression with the jury. He'd said you should get your hair cut before court. He wanted you to look like a fuckin' preppie in an orange jumpsuit. You disregarded all of that advice.

But, for some reason you couldn't quite put your finger on, this new advice hit home. You didn't want to take more medicine, of course. Was it even *possible* to dope you up more than you'd already been doped up? That's not the part of the advice that seemed helpful. No, it was the other part: "They aren't going to let someone who's actively psychotic around a rug rat." You had to start paying attention to how crazy you came across because if you seemed too crazy, they'd never let you see your kid.

You looked Public Defender Ken in the eyes. "I'll act normal," you said, with conviction. It felt odd, to aspire to normality. It was an aspiration you hadn't had since you were eight or nine.

Public Defender Ken fist-bumped you again. "Respect, bro, respect. Oh, and you might want to write Ms. Petridis and find out if she's willing to testify on your behalf." He then went to his plastic briefcase and retrieved a rubbery piece of paper. "And here's a consent form for a paternity test. Could you do me a solid and sign and date it at the bottom? This way we can get the ball rolling on this part of your defense." He handed you a pen.

From the shadows under the table, the voice: "What the fuck

do you think you're doing, bucko? Why do you even care if the kid's yours or not? We're gonna fix things, real soon, so you can get out of here and cross over The Border Crossing. I've been busy speaking to thousands of others, since I last spoke to you. But, trust me: you'll be un-born. As a natural consequence, any child of yours will be, too. All of this. Doesn't. Fucking. Matter."

From next to you, a dull, molded plastic stare. Then the surfer voice. "Well, what are you waiting on, bro?"

You ran your plastic hand through your yarn/hair. You wanted to think this through, assemble a thorough list of pros and cons. Make the decision on a logical basis. But you were too tired for that so you made the decision on a basis that was far more dubious: the Great Dark Mouth was insubstantial—a voice with no physical presence. Public Defender Ken, on the other hand, was a physical entity fashioned in a crude facsimile of a fellow-member of your species. There was something in the fabric of your DNA—a sort of social mammal reflex—that made you feel more accountable to this effigy than to a mere disembodied voice (no matter how "grand" He'd been described as, no matter how often He'd been described as a "king").

Your signature on the form was twisted by your fatigue. An ugly, gnarled mess. Misshapen. But it served its purpose.

The Great Dark Mouth went on a predictable rant, after you signed it. You can't recall all that was said. You stumbled away from the conference room. Stumbled into your bed. Fell asleep on its plastic mattress.

XIX

You'd lingered so long at Step Two that even your *dreams* became infected with Plastic-Vision.

You were back in the vast desert, in the middle of the circle of towering, rotting flesh obelisks held together by a mortar of blood and shit. There were still four suns. You were still bathed in shadows.

But it was all plastic.

Moreover, a catastrophe had occurred. Cartoony fire consumed the base of each obelisk, spewing black-cotton plumes of smoke into the air. You coughed. Put your fingers under your glasses to rub your googly eyes. But you didn't fear for your safety. In the shadows, in the dark, you felt protected. You knew you were dreaming. You knew you were there with the Mouth, and you were being educated. No physical harm could come to you. You were there to observe.

The pieces of plastic flesh at the bottom of each pillar shriveled in the fire, fell in on themselves, bubbled and stretched and melted and adhered to one another in a new, even-more-monstrous anatomy. An eternal coitus. Phallic intestines and waiting cavities, thrusting hands and labia-like wounds, all of them fused together by the fire's heat.

Then the bases of the pillars blackened. Began to disintegrate. Turned to ash. There was a thudding and swooshing sound as the bases of all the obelisks collapsed.

But the obelisks didn't fall. They merely shortened. It was as though each obelisk was a monumental cigarette facing burning-tip-down into the sand. They kept burning and shortening, burning and shortening.

And at the top of each obelisk, there was a crying and mewing as the sexual process bore fruit. Litters of tiny, plastic baby doll hands skittered, spider-like, out of filthy, decaying plastic mouths and birth canals and anuses and wounds. Tiny plastic baby doll tongues slithered out like worms. Tiny plastic baby doll hearts rolled out. And then the cycle continued as *they* began to copulate with one another, thus insuring the continued existence of the pillars.

Then the Great Dark Mouth spoke. "You were disturbed when you saw your reflection in jail, bucko. Think of this as another disturbing reflection. Another reminder of who and what you are. You copulated. And I'll tell you that which your lawyer is curious to know; that which you already know in the marrow of your bones: you *inseminated*. I can sense when the burden of new life grows like a barnacle on the universe. I can see in the darkness of the womb. The child in Cressida's belly bears your likeness.

"You committed yourself to continuing the hideous chain, making sure the tower is never consumed. You played a part in creating a being who will one day be nothing but a corpse. But before it becomes a corpse, it will be a thing possessed by *the fear* it will become a corpse. It will cry in its hospice bed for fear of the end and the pain that comes with the end. For fear that it'll have to leave everyone. But before it cries in its hospice bed, it will cry in its crib. It will wail for fear of starvation. Fear will be the only constant in its life. Love comes and goes. Only fear abides.

"This is what you did, when you thrust your flesh-thing in the cripple's cunt! You devolved to the most depraved beast.

"But there's hope, bucko. Tomorrow, you will meet another of my disciples. One who does my will in the flesh-world. You will know him when you see him. He will arrange for your escape. From the hospital. From life. He will take you to the retrieve a new passport. He's been instructed to assist you rob your mother's grave, if necessary. He'll then transport you to the new location of The Border Crossing. There, your existence will be erased like the error it was. All *consequences* of your existence will be erased. Your foul misdeed of procreation will be erased.

"Now wake up and perform the magick. Go get another passport. Proceed along the Three-Fold Path. Then, and only then, will you be ready for un-birth. So... go! Wake!"

And then you felt the sweet breeze of oblivion blow through you. It whipped up the fire, speeding along the disintegration of each base. The plastic pieces at the top of the obelisks quickened the rate of their rutting to keep up.

XX

You didn't know what time it was when you woke up. Judging by the commotion at the nurse's station you thought it might be around shift change. Close to seven in the morning. They didn't let you have a room with a window or a clock, so you couldn't be sure. If you wanted to know for sure, you'd have to walk out to the nurse's station. A clock had been mounted on the wall there. But you just didn't have the energy.

It wasn't that the dream paralyzed you with fear. It had frightening images, but its cumulative effect wasn't one of fright.

No, its cumulative effect was to trigger a deluge of self-disgust. You hadn't been able to resist the awesomely-fuckable-deformity of Cressida Petridis. And *that's* what paralyzed you: the knowledge of just how easily you'd succumbed to her wiles. You hadn't given any thought to the possibility of her becoming pregnant. Neither of you had. But that was the consequence.

You knew how much you'd hated life, pretty much since you were ten. And yet, you'd taken no precautions against creating *another* life who would be expected to go through the same misery. Who knows—maybe even *worse* misery.

What sort of mother would Cressida prove to be? Hell,

for that matter, would your offspring have to go around on crutches, too? You never found out why she'd had to use them. Was it an accommodation she'd needed to cope with a genetic condition or with injuries from an accident? What would happen when other kids found out you were its father? News cameras had been around to film you each time you'd entered and left the courthouse. You'd acquired a certain amount of notoriety (how much, you weren't certain, but *enough*). Would your child be teased because of your escapades? Would they interfere with your child's ability to find a comfortable place on the ladder? Would there be other jocks who would place other bags of rotting sandwiches and sour milk on other chairs? Would your child have other lost friendships? Other failed attempts at connection with fellow-students and teachers alike?

Would its surviving grandparents (on either side) raise it? You found that prospect particularly sickening. Or, maybe instead of raising it they'd pressure Cressida to give the child up for adoption? Would you even be consulted, if that was the case?

Did you even care?

Did you *want* your child to have a place on the ladder?

What *did* you want for your child?

If such a situation had been presented to you as a hypothetical, a year ago, the answer would have been simple: sweet, numb oblivion. Abortion, if not un-birth by way of the Mouth. But there was nothing hypothetical about it now. There was a being in Cressida's belly. Against all odds, Cressida had looked *happy* with a being in her belly. If you took the help that the Mouth promised would arrive today; if you walked into the Black Room at The Border Crossing, passport in hand, then your existence and all its consequences would be undone. You'd be un-born. In the process, your child would be un-conceived.

Is that what you wanted?

Logic seemed to suggest that, yes, that's exactly what you wanted.

But logic, in this situation, was a farce. You were a plastic doll with yarn for hair. You giggled softly to yourself when you thought about how all of this must look. A doll attempting to rationally analyze pros and cons, as though there was something important and meaningful going on up in its plastic noggin. As though it was a real boy.

There was an arrogance and sense of entitlement inseparable from that train of thought.

You were an unreal entity. Just a doll. What business did you have analyzing things? Logic wasn't your birthright.

***

The Mouth's minion showed up much later that day. Toward the end of the afternoon. Through the filter of Plastic-Vision, he looked like an evil wizard action figure holding a plastic briefcase. He was introduced to you as Dr. Hatton, a licensed psychologist who was there to give you court-ordered personality tests. But as soon as you saw the black animals emblazoned on his blue hat and robes, you knew that wasn't the true reason for his appearance. The snake, the spider, the horse, the crow: you'd seen them before, at The Border Crossing. These were, in some way, associated with the Mouth. His totems. His avatars.

The wizard-shrink took you to a private consulting room. Put his plastic briefcase to the side. "I really am a psychologist," he said in a voice sounding like Gargamel's. "That's why they let me in here. The Mouth summoned me shortly after you were captured. It has taken me some time to become hired by the hospital. That's the cause of the delay. Of course, as soon as they find out that I've assisted with your escape, we'll both be fugitives. And that's going to complicate matters. It's an unfortunate thing, that they made you scrub your mother's blood off your hand after they collected a sample for evidence. Now we're going to have to collect a new passport. Not that I'm complaining, mind you. I'm happy to serve the Mouth.

"I used to just be an ordinary psychologist, you know. Preaching the value of life to clients who knew better. Spouting any shred of nonsense to keep them from killing themselves. You see, I wanted to prevent suicides because my brother-in-law had committed suicide. I saw how it impacted my sister. But then I received the Revelation of the Mouth. I saw there was another way. A way to end existence without upsetting anyone else. A Path to un-birth.

"That's when I became a double agent, so to speak. Undercover behind enemy lines, you might say. I operate in the flesh world, doing things that the Mouth Himself is too ethereal to do. I have a key to the unit. Just follow me and do what I say."

Like everyone else in the world, you've resisted doing things that people said you should do. You were feeling the pressure now. Accountability. The Mouth in the flesh, so to speak, through His representative. And yet, it was all too much. The wizard get-up, the Gargamel voice. Plastic this and plastic that. Digging people up, taking bits of their flesh. Going to The Border Crossing.

So much work. Too much work, given that you were no longer certain it was what you wanted. Cressida had showed up in court, after all. Had called your name. She'd wanted to talk to you. Maybe she would try to see you there at the hospital, after you were cleared for visitors. Maybe one day you would see your baby. Maybe it wouldn't have the same problems you'd had.

It was hard, so hard, to confide all of this in the Ambassador of the Mouth. But you did it. It may have been the most courageous thing you've ever done. Or the most foolish.

"So… all these months of preparation," the wizard-shrink-Ambassador said, "for nothing. Do you realize the *gift* that you're talking about throwing away? Do you realize how much some of us would give to be deemed fascinating enough for consumption? To be Chosen? That fucking cripple and the fucking baby in her womb are enough to make you renounce Him?"

"It's a lot of things," you admitted. "It's Cressida, sure. It's the baby. It was kind of fucked up, but Cressida looked happy— really, honestly *happy* in the courtroom. Happy to be there and see me. Maybe even happy to be pregnant with my kid. And, if you think about it, *who else* is going to get her pregnant? All the other boys called her names. They don't see what I see in her. So this might be her only chance to be a mom. And I think she actually enjoys all the attention the trial has brought to me. I think she likes the drama. I think it, in a weird way, makes her feel normal—a part of things. I don't think she ever had that feeling before.

"If I go through un-birth, then all of that will be taken away from her. I can make the decision in favor of oblivion for myself. But now that also means making it for someone else, too. Two someone elses, really. I don't know if I should do that or not. I mean, you've got to admit, it complicates things."

"It complicates nothing. It magnifies the error of your existence. Doubles it: now *two* lives full of misery where only one stood before, as I'm sure your child's life will be every bit as wretched as its father's. Makes it all the more regrettable, makes things so much *simpler*."

"That makes sense."

"So come with me, if it makes sense."

But there was something inside of you that didn't care if it made sense. Maybe the *something* was that part of you that always wanted some connection to the world, but wouldn't admit it to yourself. The part of you that knew that once the baby was born, you'd always be its father. That no one could ever take that away from you. That once the baby was born, Cressida would always be its mother, and that no one could take *that* away from *her*.

Or maybe that something was far less admirable: the part of you hell-bent on self-sabotage. The part of you that could never see any project through to its completion. The part of you that insisted on doing the wrong thing *because* it was the wrong thing.

Or maybe it was sheer lust: it had been so long since you'd gotten laid. You had to hold on to hope—however distant— that one day you might thrust your cock once again into Cressida's cunt while clawing your fingernails into her shoulders. After all of this, it wasn't likely you'd have many other takers.

You shook your head. "I'm not coming with you. I'm tempted to leave with you, just to escape and go off somewhere on the streets and hide. But what sort of life would that be? Always on the run. Lots of stress. I'm *done* with stress, you know. Besides, if I did that there wouldn't be much hope of hearing about my kid."

"I wouldn't help you escape, just to escape. If you tried anything like that, I'd drag your ass back here. I'll only help you get out of here so you can complete the Three-Fold Path. I'm not interested in aiding and abetting any old mundane escape attempt."

"Then I'm definitely not interested. I'm going to see the legal process through. I've done a lot of things that could get me in serious trouble, but they're not charging me with those things. They don't know about those things. They're only charging me with killing my mom. And I didn't kill my mom. The trial will prove that. Everything's gonna be okay."

"You fool! You don't realize that once you renounce the Mouth, He will never again consider you for devouring. You will be like unto poison to Him—poison, that He was considering eating but didn't. The mere sight of you will be like unto vomit to the Mouth. All this business about Cressida and the baby. Jesus Christ, it's the schmaltziest thing I've heard in a long, long time. So that's what you're telling me—love conquers all?"

"Not love," you said. Maybe it was, but you didn't *think* so. "I dunno, lust? That old desire for ownership of her twisted body. Along with just liking being connected for a change, you know? She could make all the difference for me. She and that baby. They could save my life, in more ways than one."

"Do you really buy the line you attorney is selling you, about her testimony maybe turning around your case? I've read your file. The deck is stacked against you. You have a documented history of past violence against your mother. Your own fucking *brother* will testify that you'd wanted to kill her. For every Cressida who testifies on your behalf, twenty other kids and teachers will testify against you. Tell the court you were a loner and a freak. Then, Officer Collins will testify against you. That will pretty much nail it.

"If you renounce the Mouth, you'll only live long enough to see the appeals process go through. And I can guaran-fucking-tee you Cressida won't stay loyal to you through that. She's going to need a man who can bring in some money to support her. And you'll die like a dog. You'll be on a gurney and dozens of eyes will be glaring at you as the lethal injection is brought in. And your death will be nothing but a hollow ceremony. A public humiliation. A warning to others to not go all squishy-gushy. But, of course, it's a warning that won't work because those sorts of warnings never work. And you'll feel terror at the whole thing. Terror you can avoid by just following me. You dolt, can't you see I'm trying to convince you to do *what's best*."

You wanted him to shut up. You hated his Gargamel voice and his plastic blue robes and the stupid black animals. You were tired and just wanted to go back to your room. So you said the words that you knew would end it all. Spit them out as quickly as you could, through the haze of sedation. "I re-nounce the Great Dark Mouth. I renounce the Black Room. I renounce the Gift of Plastic-Vision. I renounce *Perfect Monsters*. I renounce derangement."

And then a cold, wild wind gusted through the meeting room, howling and tearing the plastic world apart. Flaying the plastic off of you and making it part of the whirlwind. Flaying the plastic off *everything* and making it part of the whirlwind.

You feared for your life, and realized how odd it felt to fear for your life. You covered your head with your arms. Fell to the ground and assumed the fetal position.

Bits of plastic whipped against you in the whirlwind, cutting your arms. The wind pounded your bones. Dr. Hatton's brief-case thudded against something. The table keeled over. All the chairs rattled against the wall, against each other, against the fallen table. The footfalls of heavy shoes fell outside the confer-ence room door. You heard knocking.

The wind stopped.

When you looked up, Dr. Hatton was no longer a plastic wizard action figure. He was a tall, thin bearded man around forty, wearing gray slacks and a blue dress shirt and a white necktie. An abstract black pattern was printed on his tie, and—looking closely—you could see the Four Totems of the Mouth inside of it.

He towered over your cowering body. Opened the door.

An orderly (an honest-to-god, *flesh-and-blood* orderly) stepped through. "What's going on in here?"

Dr. Hatton glared at you. "I was evaluating the patient, asking him questions. He began to give very strange and unfortunate responses. The next thing I knew, the chairs were all over the place."

"Okay, mister," the orderly said, "let's get you back to the nurse's station for another shot. Get those cuts on your arms cleaned up. How the hell did you manage to do *that* to yourself? You use the bottom of a chair leg? You smuggle some contraband in there? I'll have to search you. You folks are inventive as hell, I'll give you that!"

You didn't fight him. There was, in fact, something pleasurable and soothing about the sensation of his fleshy hand on your fleshy shoulder as he led you away. The Gift of Plastic-Vision had been removed from you. Things now looked and felt the way they had before.

The whole thing felt so good, so *right*, it gave you goosebumps. You felt like you imagined one of those tugboats in the Ohio River felt after it returned to port. There was a sense, inside yourself, of reattachment. Reconnection. It wasn't that you were returning to your old life. Too much had happened for that to be the case. But you were returning to life, itself.

As the orderly led you away to the nurse's station, the head psychiatrist passed you. He was on the way to confer with Dr. Hatton. You overheard him ask about the test results.

"He's the most insane person I've ever met," Dr. Hatton replied.

XXI

There were people who said you were insane and there were people who said you were only *pretending* to be insane to avoid having to go to trial. There were people who said that even if you were insane, you should be killed because of the menace you posed to society.

There were people who didn't think you posed a menace to society, but thought you should be killed for other reasons. Once you overheard nurses talking about threatened lay-offs at the hospital due to budget cuts. One of them said that you should be killed because it cost too much to feed you and clothe you and put a roof over your head. If only you (and patients like you) weren't there, then the state would have enough money to avoid cutbacks. A second nurse told the first nurse that that was a stupid line of reasoning. If there were fewer patients at the hospital then they'd cut back even more. No, the second nurse said, there should be *more* patients, not fewer. They should cut back *some other* hospital. Not yours. Kill *some other* psycho. Not you (although, the second nurse admitted, it was totally *understandable* that the first nurse wanted you dead).

Everyone there at the hospital had an opinion about you, and that opinion usually wasn't kind. Even the other patients didn't like you. That came as a surprise. They were, after all, folks cut from the same cloth as you. Some of them proudly proclaimed their offenses. They were rapists, arsonists, pedophiles. Like you, they weren't the greatest enthusiasts of hygiene. They had tangled, unkempt hair and bleary eyes.

And yet, even *they* gave you a wide berth when you walked out of your room to get your meal tray. Just like everyone in high school did in the cafeteria.

And Cressida—Jesus, Cressida. Of course, the paternity test verified you were the father. She sent you a few letters, after finding out the results. Letters telling you that she honestly didn't know what she was going to do, that she'd hid the pregnancy from everyone for as long as she could because she didn't know what to do. Letters saying that she hadn't really enjoyed your time together as a couple, but that maybe this could be a new beginning. Maybe—with this child; with this *boy* she was carrying—your life wouldn't be a total failure. Maybe—once your son was born—she would send pictures. She said her due date was June 27th.

***

Her last letter came on July 3rd. There was a baby picture along with it. He looked like you. *Exactly* like you. And that's when you knew you'd made the right decision. It was like another *you* had been brought into the world. It was like getting a second chance.

But there was something amiss. She told you the baby's weight and height, but she didn't tell you his name. Then came the hammer.

Cressida said her parents had indeed persuaded her to give the child up for adoption. She'd finally agreed to it the night before she went into labor. They'd called an adoption agency and had everything worked out at the hospital for an emergency placement.

She said it was going to be a "closed" adoption. The adoption agency would never reveal the identity of the adoptive parents to her. They would never reveal your identity or hers to the adoptive parents, either. Something about that seemed unfair, to everyone. It didn't seem right. But nobody gave two fucks about what was right.

You wondered how you could be cut out of that decision. Had there been legal maneuvering you hadn't been informed about, on the grounds that telling you would be against your own best interests? Was it the insanity thing? Did some doctor sign a paper saying you were incompetent to make legal decisions regarding adoption?

You asked to use the phone at the nurse's station to call your public defender. You got voice mail. You left five messages. He never called you back. It turned out he'd quit being a public defender shortly after your last meeting and you'd been assigned a new lawyer—a lady who said she was just there to represent you for the murder case and that adoption law was outside her scope of practice. You'd have to hire a second lawyer out of pocket if you wanted help on that front.

What were you to make of things? You had a son who would forever be a cipher. What sort of family would he end up with? What would his life be like? Would his parents ever disclose the adoption? Would he go looking for his roots someday and find out about you in the process? Would you still be alive at the time?

You didn't know. You just knew you had the picture and that it revealed him to be flesh and blood, not plastic. *Your* flesh and blood. And you found that to be something to celebrate.

You vowed that, from then on, you'd be the model prisoner/ patient. You'd cooperate. Be as normal as possible. You'd say "Yes, ma'am" and "Yes, sir" to the doctors and nurses. You'd respect their authority over you.

This approach reaped its rewards. The head psychiatrist met with you one day and commented on your "improved adjust- ment to the milieu". He said there was a calisthenics class held each morning in the hospital gymnasium. Said you could, perhaps, join in. He could sign a doctor's order granting this privilege. If you acted up, it would be taken away from you.

"If you agree to join in on these classes, it'll get the other patients used to seeing you around and not just in your room all the time. Then maybe they won't be so frightened of you. It'll be good for your health. Good for your mood, too. Good all around. And it will certainly look good, to the court, if you show them you're fully participating with your treatment plan. Then they can't say that you aren't at least *trying* to get better. They can't say you're faking being sick."

You nodded. "I'd like to enroll in the class, sir. Oh thank you, sir. Thank you."

***

"Calisthenics class" was less appealing than it initially sound- ed. There were a dozen of you in the "class". You were accom- panied by a dozen orderlies. There were basketball hoops in the gym, but you didn't use them. All you did was walk around its perimeter, like old people at the mall. You were sedated, so it wasn't like you could run. But you would have liked to do more than just walk. You would have liked to have played a game.

One of the other patients (an old dude with a white goatee)

complained. "It's too long a walk. It's the Bataan Death March, I tells ya. The Bataan Death March!"

You realized that was a negative way of thinking. You told him so. "It's not a death march, it's good exercise. It's just what the doctor ordered! It's just a wee merry stroll. What day is this? Is it July fourth? It must be close. We can pretend we're having a parade!"

The orderlies smiled at you. Giggled in surprise at your enthusiasm in offering up a fun way of reframing the exercise. "That's right, fellas," one of them said. "It's your parade. Let's pretend you're downtown, marching with the Shriners and the high school bands."

And then you hummed "The Stars and Stripes Forever." You didn't get it one hundred percent right. You missed notes. You were sleepy from your morning meds. But you came *close enough* to getting it right that everyone else knew what you were driving at. It started to catch on, beginning with the old man who'd been so whiny before. He hummed, and his humming seemed to put a little spring in his step. Before you knew it, *all* the rapists, arsonists, and pedophiles in front of you and behind you had started to hum along, too, as they marched.

Acknowledgments

This book is indebted to the work of Edgar Allan Poe (in particular, his concept of "the imp of the perverse"). My thanks to all the teachers in Cecil County, Maryland, in the '80s (their names, sadly, long-swept from memory), who first exposed me to Poe's work and arranged for a gaggle of us rural kids to visit Baltimore's Poe house. Thanks to the actor who showed up that day and performed his Poe impersonation for us. These may seem like relatively small (or even silly) things, but they stoked my childhood imagination.

This book is also indebted to the nihilistic tag-team of Thomas Ligotti and David Benatar. I'm honestly not sure *Mr. Suicide* would exist without their pioneering work on anti-natalism. (I leave it to them to sort out their feelings about the irony of anti-natalism giving birth to new authors and books.) Likewise, I'm not sure this book would exist without Jack Ketchum and the late Richard Laymon. Laymon's books were the first to offer me the simple (but important) assurance that it was okay to use deeply taboo words in fiction. Ketchum taught me that extreme horror need not trivialize or sensationalize its subject matter; that extreme horror is just another way of being honest with the reader about how the world (at its worst) really works.

Thanks to everyone who worked in the trenches with me on this one, too. Thanks to the always-reliable Allen Griffin for his work as a beta reader. Thanks to Ross Lockhart for his invaluable editing insight. Thanks to my friends and readers who provided encouragement (either in person or online). Thanks to my husband for always being in my corner.

Finally, thanks to everyone who got me through adolescence and other rough patches in my life. Your voices have always been louder, clearer, and—ultimately—more convincing than Mr. Suicide's.

TITLES AVAILABLE FROM WORD HORDE

Tales of Jack the Ripper
an anthology edited by Ross E. Lockhart

We Leave Together
a Dogsland novel by J. M. McDermott

*The Children of Old Leech: A Tribute to the
Carnivorous Cosmos of Laird Barron*
an anthology edited by Ross E. Lockhart and Justin Steele

Vermilion
a novel by Molly Tanzer

Giallo Fantastique
an anthology edited by Ross E. Lockhart

Mr. Suicide
a novel by Nicole Cushing

Cthulhu Fhtagn! (August 2015)
an anthology edited by Ross E. Lockhart

Painted Monsters (October 2015)
a collection by Orrin Grey

Furnace (February 2016)
a collection by Livia Llewellyn

Ask for Word Horde books by name at your favorite bookseller.
Or order online at www.WordHorde.com

"A lavish, sumptuous tapestry of luxurious surrealism and strangeness."
—*The Horror Fiction Review*

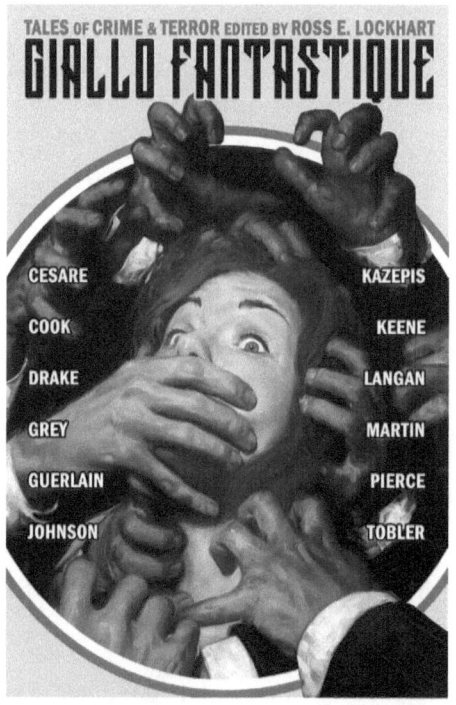

TALES OF CRIME & TERROR EDITED BY ROSS E. LOCKHART
GIALLO FANTASTIQUE

CESARE	KAZEPIS
COOK	KEENE
DRAKE	LANGAN
GREY	MARTIN
GUERLAIN	PIERCE
JOHNSON	TOBLER

AN ANTHOLOGY OF ORIGINAL STRANGE STORIES at the intersection of crime, terror, and supernatural fiction. Inspired by and drawing from the highly stylized cinematic thrillers of Argento, Bava, and Fulci; American noir and crime fiction; and the grim fantasies of Edgar Allan Poe, Guy de Maupassant, and Jean Ray, *Giallo Fantastique* seeks to unnerve readers through virtuoso storytelling and startlingly colorful imagery.

What's your favorite shade of yellow?

Trade Paperback, 240 pp, $15.99
ISBN-13: 978-1-939905-06-2
http://www.wordhorde.com

In his house at R'lyeh, Cthulhu waits dreaming...

WHAT ARE THE DREAMS THAT MONSTERS DREAM? When will the stars grow right? Where are the sunken temples in which the dreamers dwell? How will it all change when they come home?

Within these pages lie the answers, and more, in all-new stories by many of the brightest lights in dark fiction. Gathered together by Ross E. Lockhart, the editor who brought you *The Book of Cthulhu*, *The Children of Old Leech*, and *Giallo Fantastique*, *Cthulhu Fhtagn!* features nineteen weird tales inspired by H. P. Lovecraft.

Format: Trade Paperback, 324 pp, $19.99

ISBN-13: 978-1-939905-13-0

http://www.wordhorde.com

About the Author

Shirley Jackson Award finalist Nicole Cushing has written multiple stand-alone novellas and dozens of short stories. Her work has been praised by the pop culture websites Ain't It Cool News and Famous Monsters of Filmland. Several of her stories have been selected as honorable mentions (long list) for Ellen Datlow's *Best Horror of the Year* series. Her first full-length short story collection, *The Mirrors*, is also slated for publication in 2015.

A native of Maryland, she now lives with her husband in Indiana. She's active online and welcomes contact with readers via Facebook, Twitter, or (if one must be old fashioned about it) email at nicolecushingwriter@gmail.com.